The Sandman—Der Sandmann
E.T.A. Hoffmann

and

The Tales of Hoffmann Act II
Les contes d'Hoffmann Acte II
Jacques Offenbach

English-German/English-French
Parallel Text Edition

Complete and Unabridged

BILINGUAL LIBRARY

The Sandman—Der Sandmann
E.T.A. Hoffmann

and

The Tales of Hoffmann Act II
Les contes d'Hoffmann Acte II
Jacques Offenbach

**English-German/English-French
Parallel Text Edition**

Translated by J.T. Bealby (from the German)
and Charles Alfred Byrne (from the French)

Complete and Unabridged
Edited with an introduction by D. Bannon

BILINGUAL LIBRARY

The Sandman—Der Sandmann and The Tales of Hoffmann—Les contes d'Hoffmann: English-German/English-French Parallel Text Edition

Cover painting: *Nachtmahr* by Johann Heinrich Füssli (1781)

The Sandman—Der Sandmann was first published in a book of short stories entitles *Night Pieces—Nachtstücke* in 1817.

Jacques Offenbach's *The Tales of Hoffmann—Les Contes d'Hoffmann* French libretto by Jules Barbier premiered in Paris in 1881.

The Bilingual Library parallel text edition of *The Sandman—Der Sandmann* uses the J.T. Bealby translation originally published in Weird Tales Volume One by Charles Scribner's Sons in 1885.

The Bilingual Library uses the Charles Alfred Byrne English translation of *The Tales of Hoffmann—Les Contes d'Hoffmann* as it was performed in the Manhattan Opera House under the direction of Oscar Hammerstein and published by Steinway & Sons in 1907.

Unless otherwise noted, photographs in *The Tales of Hoffmann—Les Contes d'Hoffmann* are from the 2008 Boston Lyric Opera production of *Les contes d'Hoffmann* as conducted by Keith Lockhart. Production shots by Jeffrey Dunn © 2008.

First Bilingual Library Parallel Text Edition, 2010

ISBN: 978-0-557-43089-5

BILINGUAL LIBRARY

CONTENTS

The Sandman—Der Sandmann

I n t r o d u c t i o n

The Bilingual Library parallel text edition of *The Sandman—Der Sandmann* uses the J.T. Bealby translation originally published in *Weird Tales Volume One* by Charles Scribner's Sons in 1885. The German text was first published in a book of short stories entitles *Night Pieces—Nachtstücke* in 1817. Hoffmann's disturbing tale has informed much of modern horror. The Bilingual Library presents the libretto of one of the most famous adaptations, Jacques Offenbach's *The Tales of Hoffmann—Les contes d'Hoffmann*. This volume uses the Charles Alfred Byrne English translation as it was performed in the Manhattan Opera House under the direction of Oscar Hammerstein and published by Steinway & Sons in 1907. The French text uses the Jules Barbier libretto from the Paris premiere in 1881.

Fiction is translated by paragraph. Line-by-line translations are often cumbersome and sometimes nonsensical. When a character is discussing a point within a paragraph, the translator may choose to shorten the phrasing by referring to the main point with a pronoun after it has been introduced or by allowing the context to imply meaning. Ultimately the translator must balance the tone and style of the prose with the intent of the dramatic moment. This ensures contextual accuracy and a uniform tone. To help readers enjoy the short story in both languages, The Bilingual Library rarely breaks paragraphs between pages. Discrepancies in placement have been adjusted to the German text.

Illustrations for *The Sandman—Der Sandmann* were taken from work representative of the period and the content. Unless otherwise noted, photographs in *The Tales of Hoffmann—Les contes d'Hoffmann* are from the 2008 Boston Lyric Opera production of *Les contes d'Hoffmann* as conducted by Keith Lockhart. Production shots by Jeffrey Dunn © 2008.

Translation is adaptation. In serving the reader and the original text, translators struggle with what is lost between context and literal meaning. Yet in the process something new is gained—a translated novel. The Bilingual Library is designed to help readers discover the rich prose of both worlds.

D. Bannon
The Bilingual Library

E.T.A. Hoffmann (1776-1822)

THE
SANDMAN

E.T.A. HOFFMANN

DER
SANDMANN

NATHANAEL TO LOTHAIR

I know you are all very uneasy because I have not written for such a long, long time. Mother, to be sure, is angry, and Clara, I dare say, believes I am living here in riot and revelry, and quite forgetting my sweet angel, whose image is so deeply engraved upon my heart and mind. But that is not so; daily and hourly do I think of you all, and my lovely Clara's form comes to gladden me in my dreams, and smiles upon me with her bright eyes, as graciously as she used to do in the days when I went in and out amongst you. Oh! how could I write to you in the distracted state of mind in which I have been, and which, until now, has quite bewildered me! A terrible thing has happened to me. Dark forebodings of some awful fate threatening me are spreading themselves out over my head like black clouds, impenetrable to every friendly ray of sunlight. I must now tell you what has taken place; I must, that I see well enough, but only to think upon it makes the wild laughter burst from my lips. Oh! my dear, dear Lothair, what shall I say to make you feel, if only in an inadequate way, that that which happened to me a few days ago could thus really exercise such a hostile and disturbing influence upon my life? Oh that you were here to see for yourself! but now you will, I suppose, take me for a superstitious ghost-seer. In a word, the terrible thing which I have experienced, the fatal effect of which I in vain exert every effort to shake off, is simply that some days ago, namely, on the 30th October, at twelve o'clock at noon, a dealer in weather-glasses came into my room and wanted to sell me one of his wares. I bought nothing, and threatened to kick him downstairs, whereupon he went away of his own accord.

You will conclude that it can only be very peculiar relations—relations intimately intertwined with my life—that can give significance to this event, and that it must be the person of this unfortunate hawker which has had such a very inimical effect upon me. And so it really is. I will summon up all my faculties in order to narrate to you calmly and patiently as much of the early days of my youth as will suffice to put matters before you in such a way that your keen sharp intellect may grasp everything clearly and distinctly, in bright and living pictures. Just as I am beginning, I hear you laugh and Clara say, "What's all this childish nonsense about!" Well, laugh at me, laugh heartily at me, pray do. But, good God! my hair is standing on end, and I seem to be entreating you to laugh at me in the same sort of frantic despair in which Franz Moor entreated Daniel to laugh him to scorn. But to my story.

Except at dinner we, i.e., I and my brothers and sisters, saw but little of our father all day long. His business no doubt took up most of his time. After our evening meal, which, in accordance with an old custom, was served at seven o'clock, we all went, mother with us, into father's room, and took our places around a round table. My father smoked his pipe, drinking a large glass of beer to it. Often he told us many wonderful stories, and got so excited over them that his pipe always went out; I used then to light it for him with a spill, and this formed my chief amusement.

Nathanael an Lothar

Gewiß seid Ihr alle voll Unruhe, daß ich so lange - lange nicht geschrieben. Mutter zürnt wohl, und Clara mag glauben, ich lebe hier in Saus und Braus und vergesse mein holdes Engelsbild, so tief mir in Herz und Sinn eingeprägt, ganz und gar. - Dem ist aber nicht so; täglich und stündlich gedenke ich Eurer aller und in süßen Träumen geht meines holden Clärchens freundliche Gestalt vorüber und lächelt mich mit ihren hellen Augen so anmutig an, wie sie wohl pflegte, wenn ich zu Euch hineintrat. - Ach wie vermochte ich denn Euch zu schreiben, in der zerrissenen Stimmung des Geistes, die mir bisher alle Gedanken verstörte! - Etwas Entsetzliches ist in mein Leben getreten! - Dunkle Ahnungen eines gräßlichen mir drohenden Geschicks breiten sich wie schwarze Wolkenschatten über mich aus, undurchdringlich jedem freundlichen Sonnenstrahl. - Nun soll ich Dir sagen, was mir widerfuhr. Ich muß es, das sehe ich ein, aber nur es denkend, lacht es wie toll aus mir heraus. - Ach mein herzlieber Lothar! wie fange ich es denn an, Dich nur einigermaßen empfinden zu lassen, daß das, was mir vor einigen Tagen geschah, denn wirklich mein Leben so feindlich zerstören konnte! Wärst Du nur hier, so könntest Du selbst schauen; aber jetzt hältst Du mich gewiß für einen aberwitzigen Geisterseher. - Kurz und gut, das Entsetzliche, was mir geschah, dessen tödlichen Eindruck zu vermeiden ich mich vergebens bemühe, besteht in nichts anderm, als daß vor einigen Tagen, nämlich am 30. Oktober mittags um 12 Uhr, ein Wetterglashändler in meine Stube trat und mir seine Ware anbot. Ich kaufte nichts und drohte, ihn die Treppe herabzuwerfen, worauf er aber von selbst fortging.

Du ahnest, daß nur ganz eigne, tief in mein Leben eingreifende Beziehungen diesem Vorfall Bedeutung geben können, ja, daß wohl die Person jenes unglückseligen Krämers gar feindlich auf mich wirken muß. So ist es in der Tat. Mit aller Kraft fasse ich mich zusammen, um ruhig und geduldig Dir aus meiner frühern Jugendzeit so viel zu erzählen, daß Deinem regen Sinn alles klar und deutlich in leuchtenden Bildern aufgehen wird. Indem ich anfangen will, höre ich Dich lachen und Clara sagen: »Das sind ja rechte Kindereien!« - Lacht, ich bitte Euch, lacht mich recht herzlich aus! - ich bitt Euch sehr! - Aber Gott im Himmel! die Haare sträuben sich mir und es ist, als flehe ich Euch an, mich auszulachen, in wahnsinniger Verzweiflung, wie Franz Moor den Daniel. - Nun fort zur Sache!

Außer dem Mittagsessen sahen wir, ich und mein Geschwister, tagüber den Vater wenig. Er mochte mit seinem Dienst viel beschäftigt sein. Nach dem Abendessen, das alter Sitte gemäß schon um sieben Uhr aufgetragen wurde, gingen wir alle, die Mutter mit uns, in des Vaters Arbeitszimmer und setzten uns um einen runden Tisch. Der Vater rauchte Tabak und trank ein großes Glas Bier dazu. Oft erzählte er uns viele wunderbare Geschichten und geriet darüber so in Eifer, daß ihm die Pfeife immer ausging, die ich, ihm brennend Papier hinhaltend, wieder anzünden mußte, welches mir denn ein Hauptspaß war.

Often, again, he would give us picture-books to look at, whilst he sat silent and motionless in his easy-chair, puffing out such dense clouds of smoke that we were all as it were enveloped in mist. On such evenings mother was very sad; and directly it struck nine she said, "Come, children! off to bed! Come! The 'Sandman' is come I see." And I always did seem to hear something trampling upstairs with slow heavy steps; that must be the Sandman. Once in particular I was very much frightened at this dull trampling and knocking; as mother was leading us out of the room I asked her, "O mamma! but who is this nasty Sandman who always sends us away from papa? What does he look like?" "There is no Sandman, my dear child," mother answered; "when I say the Sandman is come, I only mean that you are sleepy and can't keep your eyes open, as if somebody had put sand in them." This answer of mother's did not satisfy me; nay, in my childish mind the thought clearly unfolded itself that mother denied there was a Sandman only to prevent us being afraid,—why, I always heard him come upstairs. Full of curiosity to learn something more about this Sandman and what he had to do with us children, I at length asked the old woman who acted as my youngest sister's attendant, what sort of a man he was—the Sandman? "Why, 'thanael, darling, don't you know?" she replied. "Oh! he's a wicked man, who comes to little children when they won't go to bed and throws handfuls of sand in their eyes, so that they jump out of their heads all bloody; and he puts them into a bag and takes them to the half-moon as food for his little ones; and they sit there in the nest and have hooked beaks like owls, and they pick naughty little boys' and girls' eyes out with them." After this I formed in my own mind a horrible picture of the cruel Sandman. When anything came blundering upstairs at night I trembled with fear and dismay; and all that my mother could get out of me were the stammered words "The Sandman! the Sandman!" whilst the tears coursed down my cheeks. Then I ran into my bedroom, and the whole night through tormented myself with the terrible apparition of the Sandman. I was quite old enough to perceive that the old woman's tale about the Sandman and his little ones' nest in the half-moon couldn't be altogether true; nevertheless the Sandman continued to be for me a fearful incubus, and I was always seized with terror—my blood always ran cold, not only when I heard anybody come up the stairs, but when I heard anybody noisily open my father's room door and go in. Often he stayed away for a long season altogether; then he would come several times in close succession.

Oft gab er uns aber Bilderbücher in die Hände, saß stumm und starr in seinem Lehnstuhl und blies starke Dampfwolken von sich, daß wir alle wie im Nebel schwammen. An solchen Abenden war die Mutter sehr traurig und kaum schlug die Uhr neun, so sprach sie: »Nun Kinder! - zu Bette! zu Bette! der Sandmann kommt, ich merk es schon.« Wirklich hörte ich dann jedesmal etwas schweren langsamen Tritts die Treppe heraufpoltern; das mußte der Sandmann sein. Einmal war mir jenes dumpfe Treten und Poltern besonders graulich; ich frug die Mutter, indem sie uns fortführte: »Ei Mama! wer ist denn der böse Sandmann, der uns immer von Papa forttreibt? - wie sieht er denn aus?« - »Es gibt keinen Sandmann, mein liebes Kind«, erwiderte die Mutter: »wenn ich sage, der Sandmann kommt, so will das nur heißen, ihr seid schläfrig und könnt die Augen nicht offen behalten, als hätte man euch Sand hineingestreut.« - Der Mutter Antwort befriedigte mich nicht, ja in meinem kindischen Gemüt entfaltete sich deutlich der Gedanke, daß die Mutter den Sandmann nur verleugne, damit wir uns vor ihm nicht fürchten sollten, ich hörte ihn ja immer die Treppe heraufkommen. Voll Neugierde, Näheres von diesem Sandmann und seiner Beziehung auf uns Kinder zu erfahren, frug ich endlich die alte Frau, die meine jüngste Schwester wartete: was denn das für ein Mann sei, der Sandmann? »Ei Thanelchen«, erwiderte diese, »weißt du das noch nicht? Das ist ein böser Mann, der kommt zu den Kindern, wenn sie nicht zu Bett gehen wollen und wirft ihnen Händevoll Sand in die Augen, daß sie blutig zum Kopf herausspringen, die wirft er dann in den Sack und trägt sie in den Halbmond zur Atzung für seine Kinderchen; die sitzen dort im Nest und haben krumme Schnäbel, wie die Eulen, damit picken sie der unartigen Menschenkindlein Augen auf.« - Gräßlich malte sich nun im Innern mir das Bild des grausamen Sandmanns aus; sowie es abends die Treppe heraufpolterte, zitterte ich vor Angst und Entsetzen. Nichts als den unter Tränen hergestotterten Ruf. »Der Sandmann! der Sandmann! « konnte die Mutter aus mir herausbringen. Ich lief darauf in das Schlafzimmer, und wohl die ganze Nacht über quälte mich die fürchterliche Erscheinung des Sandmanns. - Schon alt genug war ich geworden, um einzusehen, daß das mit dem Sandmann und seinem Kindernest im Halbmonde, so wie es mir die Wartefrau erzählt hatte, wohl nicht ganz seine Richtigkeit haben könne; indessen blieb mir der Sandmann ein fürchterliches Gespenst, und Grauen - Entsetzen ergriff mich, wenn ich ihn nicht allein die Treppe heraufkommen, sondern auch meines Vaters Stubentür heftig aufreißen und hineintreten hörte. Manchmal blieb er lange weg, dann kam er öfter hintereinander.

This went on for years, without my being able to accustom myself to this fearful apparition, without the image of the horrible Sandman growing any fainter in my imagination. His intercourse with my father began to occupy my fancy ever more and more; I was restrained from asking my father about him by an unconquerable shyness; but as the years went on the desire waxed stronger and stronger within me to fathom the mystery myself and to see the fabulous Sandman. He had been the means of disclosing to me the path of the wonderful and the adventurous, which so easily find lodgment in the mind of the child. I liked nothing better than to hear or read horrible stories of goblins, witches, Tom Thumbs, and so on; but always at the head of them all stood the Sandman, whose picture I scribbled in the most extraordinary and repulsive forms with both chalk and coal everywhere, on the tables, and cupboard doors, and walls. When I was ten years old my mother removed me from the nursery into a little chamber off the corridor not far from my father's room. We still had to withdraw hastily whenever, on the stroke of nine, the mysterious unknown was heard in the house. As I lay in my little chamber I could hear him go into father's room, and soon afterwards I fancied there was a fine and peculiar smelling steam spreading itself through the house. As my curiosity waxed stronger, my resolve to make somehow or other the Sandman's acquaintance took deeper root. Often when my mother had gone past, I slipped quickly out of my room into the corridor, but I could never see anything, for always before I could reach the place where I could get sight of him, the Sandman was well inside the door. At last, unable to resist the impulse any longer, I determined to conceal myself in father's room and there wait for the Sandman.

One evening I perceived from my father's silence and mother's sadness that the Sandman would come; accordingly, pleading that I was excessively tired, I left the room before nine o'clock and concealed myself in a hiding-place close beside the door. The street door creaked, and slow, heavy, echoing steps crossed the passage towards the stairs. Mother hurried past me with my brothers and sisters. Softly—softly—I opened father's room door. He sat as usual, silent and motionless, with his back towards it; he did not hear me; and in a moment I was in and behind a curtain drawn before my father's open wardrobe, which stood just inside the room. Nearer and nearer and nearer came the echoing footsteps. There was a strange coughing and shuffling and mumbling outside. My heart beat with expectation and fear. A quick step now close, close beside the door, a noisy rattle of the handle, and the door flies open with a bang. Recovering my courage with an effort, I take a cautious peep out. In the middle of the room in front of my father stands the Sandman, the bright light of the lamp falling full upon his face. The Sandman, the terrible Sandman, is the old advocate Coppelius who often comes to dine with us.

Jahrelang dauerte das, und nicht gewöhnen konnte ich mich an den unheimlichen Spuk, nicht bleicher wurde in mir das Bild des grausigen Sandmanns. Sein Umgang mit dem Vater fing an meine Fantasie immer mehr und mehr zu beschäftigen: den Vater darum zu befragen hielt mich eine unüberwindliche Scheu zurück, aber selbst - selbst das Geheimnis zu erforschen, den fabelhaften Sandmann zu sehen, dazu keimte mit den Jahren immer mehr die Lust in mir empor. Der Sandmann hatte mich auf die Bahn des Wunderbaren, Abenteuerlichen gebracht, das so schon leicht im kindlichen Gemüt sich einnistet. Nichts war mir lieber, als schauerliche Geschichten von Kobolten, Hexen, Däumlingen usw. zu hören oder zu lesen; aber obenan stand immer der Sandmann, den ich in den seltsamsten, abscheulichsten Gestalten überall auf Tische, Schränke und Wände mit Kreide, Kohle, hinzeichnete. Als ich zehn Jahre alt geworden, wies mich die Mutter aus der Kinderstube in ein Kämmerchen, das auf dem Korridor unfern von meines Vaters Zimmer lag. Noch immer mußten wir uns, wenn auf den Schlag neun Uhr sich jener Unbekannte im Hause hören ließ, schnell entfernen. In meinem Kämmerchen vernahm ich, wie er bei dem Vater hineintrat und bald darauf war es mir dann, als verbreite sich im Hause ein feiner seltsam riechender Dampf. Immer höher mit der Neugierde wuchs der Mut, auf irgend eine Weise des Sandmanns Bekanntschaft zu machen. Oft schlich ich schnell aus dem Kämmerchen auf den Korridor, wenn die Mutter vorübergegangen, aber nichts konnte ich erlauschen, denn immer war der Sandmann schon zur Türe hinein, wenn ich den Platz erreicht hatte, wo er mir sichtbar werden mußte. Endlich von unwiderstehlichem Drange getrieben, beschloß ich, im Zimmer des Vaters selbst mich zu verbergen und den Sandmann zu erwarten.

An des Vaters Schweigen, an der Mutter Traurigkeit merkte ich eines Abends, daß der Sandmann kommen werde; ich schützte daher große Müdigkeit vor, verließ schon vor neun Uhr das Zimmer und verbarg mich dicht neben der Türe in einen Schlupfwinkel. Die Haustür knarrte, durch den Flur ging es, langsamen, schweren, dröhnenden Schrittes nach der Treppe. Die Mutter eilte mit dem Geschwister mir vorüber. Leise - leise öffnete ich des Vaters Stubentür. Er saß, wie gewöhnlich, stumm und starr den Rücken der Türe zugekehrt, er bemerkte mich nicht, schnell war ich hinein und hinter der Gardine, die einem gleich neben der Türe stehenden offnen Schrank, worin meines Vaters Kleider hingen, vorgezogen war. - Näher - immer näher dröhnten die Tritte - es hustete und scharrte und brummte seltsam draußen. Das Herz bebte mir vor Angst und Erwartung. - Dicht, dicht vor der Türe ein scharfer Tritt - ein heftiger Schlag auf die Klinke, die Tür springt rasselnd auf! - Mit Gewalt mich ermannend gucke ich behutsam hervor. Der Sandmann steht mitten in der Stube vor meinem Vater, der helle Schein der Lichter brennt ihm ins Gesicht! - Der Sandmann, der fürchterliche Sandmann ist der alte Advokat Coppelius, der manchmal bei uns zu Mittage ißt!

But the most hideous figure could not have awakened greater trepidation in my heart than this Coppelius did. Picture to yourself a large broad-shouldered man, with an immensely big head, a face the colour of yellow-ochre, grey bushy eyebrows, from beneath which two piercing, greenish, cat-like eyes glittered, and a prominent Roman nose hanging over his upper lip. His distorted mouth was often screwed up into a malicious smile; then two dark-red spots appeared on his cheeks, and a strange hissing noise proceeded from between his tightly clenched teeth. He always wore an ash-grey coat of an old-fashioned cut, a waistcoat of the same, and nether extremities to match, but black stockings and buckles set with stones on his shoes. His little wig scarcely extended beyond the crown of his head, his hair was curled round high up above his big red ears, and plastered to his temples with cosmetic, and a broad closed hair-bag stood out prominently from his neck, so that you could see the silver buckle that fastened his folded neck-cloth. Altogether he was a most disagreeable and horribly ugly figure; but what we children detested most of all was his big coarse hairy hands; we could never fancy anything that he had once touched. This he had noticed; and so, whenever our good mother quietly placed a piece of cake or sweet fruit on our plates, he delighted to touch it under some pretext or other, until the bright tears stood in our eyes, and from disgust and loathing we lost the enjoyment of the tit-bit that was intended to please us. And he did just the same thing when father gave us a glass of sweet wine on holidays. Then he would quickly pass his hand over it, or even sometimes raise the glass to his blue lips, and he laughed quite sardonically when all we dared do was to express our vexation in stifled sobs. He habitually called us the "little brutes;" and when he was present we might not utter a sound; and we cursed the ugly spiteful man who deliberately and intentionally spoilt all our little pleasures. Mother seemed to dislike this hateful Coppelius as much as we did; for as soon as he appeared her cheerfulness and bright and natural manner were transformed into sad, gloomy seriousness. Father treated him as if he were a being of some higher race, whose ill-manners were to be tolerated, whilst no efforts ought to be spared to keep him in good-humour. He had only to give a slight hint, and his favourite dishes were cooked for him and rare wine uncorked.

As soon as I saw this Coppelius, therefore, the fearful and hideous thought arose in my mind that he, and he alone, must be the Sandman; but I no longer conceived of the Sandman as the bugbear in the old nurse's fable, who fetched children's eyes and took them to the half-moon as food for his little ones—no! but as an ugly spectre-like fiend bringing trouble and misery and ruin, both temporal and everlasting, everywhere wherever he appeared.

Aber die gräßlichste Gestalt hätte mir nicht tieferes Entsetzen erregen können, als eben dieser Coppelius. - Denke Dir einen großen breitschultrigen Mann mit einem unförmlich dicken Kopf, erdgelbem Gesicht, buschigten grauen Augenbrauen, unter denen ein Paar grünliche Katzenaugen stechend hervorfunkeln, großer, starker über die Oberlippe gezogener Nase. Das schiefe Maul verzieht sich oft zum hämischen Lachen; dann werden auf den Backen ein paar dunkelrote Flecke sichtbar und ein seltsam zischender Ton fährt durch die zusammengekniffenen Zähne. Coppelius erschien immer in einem altmodisch zugeschnittenen aschgrauen Rocke, eben solcher Weste und gleichen Beinkleidern, aber dazu schwarze Strümpfe und Schuhe mit kleinen Steinschnallen. Die kleine Perücke reichte kaum bis über den Kopfwirbel heraus, die Kleblocken standen hoch über den großen roten Ohren und ein breiter verschlossener Haarbeutel starrte von dem Nacken weg, so daß man die silberne Schnalle sah, die die gefältelte Halsbinde schloß. Die ganze Figur war überhaupt widrig und abscheulich; aber vor allem waren uns Kindern seine großen knotigten, haarigten Fäuste zuwider, so daß wir, was er damit berührte, nicht mehr mochten. Das hatte er bemerkt und nun war es seine Freude, irgend ein Stückchen Kuchen, oder eine süße Frucht, die uns die gute Mutter heimlich auf den Teller gelegt, unter diesem, oder jenem Vorwande zu berühren, daß wir, helle Tränen in den Augen, die Näscherei, der wir uns erfreuen sollten, nicht mehr genießen mochten vor Ekel und Abscheu. Ebenso machte er es, wenn uns an Feiertagen der Vater ein klein Gläschen süßen Weins eingeschenkt hatte. Dann fuhr er schnell mit der Faust herüber, oder brachte wohl gar das Glas an die blauen Lippen und lachte recht teuflisch, wenn wir unsern Ärger nur leise schluchzend äußern durften. Er pflegte uns nur immer die kleinen Bestien zu nennen; wir durften, war er zugegen, keinen Laut von uns geben und verwünschten den häßlichen, feindlichen Mann, der uns recht mit Bedacht und Absicht auch die kleinste Freude verdarb. Die Mutter schien ebenso, wie wir, den widerwärtigen Coppelius zu hassen; denn so wie er sich zeigte, war ihr Frohsinn, ihr heiteres unbefangenes Wesen umgewandelt in traurigen, düstern Ernst. Der Vater betrug sich gegen ihn, als sei er ein höheres Wesen, dessen Unarten man dulden und das man auf jede Weise bei guter Laune erhalten müsse. Er durfte nur leise andeuten und Lieblingsgerichte wurden gekocht und seltene Weine kredenzt.

Als ich nun diesen Coppelius sah, ging es grausig und entsetzlich in meiner Seele auf, daß ja niemand anders, als er, der Sandmann sein könne, aber der Sandmann war mir nicht mehr jener Popanz aus dem Ammenmärchen, der dem Eulennest im Halbmonde Kinderaugen zur Atzung holt - nein! - ein häßlicher gespenstischer Unhold, der überall, wo er einschreitet, Jammer - Not - zeitliches, ewiges Verderben bringt.

I was spell-bound on the spot. At the risk of being discovered, and, as I well enough knew, of being severely punished, I remained as I was, with my head thrust through the curtains listening. My father received Coppelius in a ceremonious manner. "Come, to work!" cried the latter, in a hoarse snarling voice, throwing off his coat. Gloomily and silently my father took off his dressing-gown, and both put on long black smock-frocks. Where they took them from I forgot to notice. Father opened the folding-doors of a cupboard in the wall; but I saw that what I had so long taken to be a cupboard was really a dark recess, in which was a little hearth. Coppelius approached it, and a blue flame crackled upwards from it. Round about were all kinds of strange utensils. Good God! as my old father bent down over the fire how different he looked! His gentle and venerable features seemed to be drawn up by some dreadful convulsive pain into an ugly, repulsive Satanic mask. He looked like Coppelius. Coppelius plied the red-hot tongs and drew bright glowing masses out of the thick smoke and began assiduously to hammer them. I fancied that there were men's faces visible round about, but without eyes, having ghastly deep black holes where the eyes should have been. "Eyes here! Eyes here!" cried Coppelius, in a hollow sepulchral voice. My blood ran cold with horror; I screamed and tumbled out of my hiding-place into the floor. Coppelius immediately seized upon me. "You little brute! You little brute!" he bleated, grinding his teeth. Then, snatching me up, he threw me on the hearth, so that the flames began to singe my hair. "Now we've got eyes—eyes—a beautiful pair of children's eyes," he whispered, and, thrusting his hands into the flames he took out some red-hot grains and was about to strew them into my eyes. Then my father clasped his hands and entreated him, saying, "Master, master, let my Nathanael keep his eyes—oh! do let him keep them." Coppelius laughed shrilly and replied, "Well then, the boy may keep his eyes and whine and pule his way through the world; but we will now at any rate observe the mechanism of the hand and the foot." And therewith he roughly laid hold upon me, so that my joints cracked, and twisted my hands and my feet, pulling them now this way, and now that, "That's not quite right altogether! It's better as it was!—the old fellow knew what he was about." Thus lisped and hissed Coppelius; but all around me grew black and dark; a sudden convulsive pain shot through all my nerves and bones; I knew nothing more.

Ich war fest gezaubert. Auf die Gefahr entdeckt, und, wie ich deutlich dachte, hart gestraft zu werden, blieb ich stehen, den Kopf lauschend durch die Gardine hervorgestreckt. Mein Vater empfing den Coppelius feierlich. »Auf! - zum Werk«, rief dieser mit heiserer, schnurrender Stimme und warf den Rock ab. Der Vater zog still und finster seinen Schlafrock aus und beide kleideten sich in lange schwarze Kittel. Wo sie die hernahmen, hatte ich übersehen. Der Vater öffnete die Flügeltür eines Wandschranks; aber ich sah, daß das, was ich solange dafür gehalten, kein Wandschrank, sondern vielmehr eine schwarze Höhlung war, in der ein kleiner Herd stand. Coppelius trat hinzu und eine blaue Flamme knisterte auf dem Herde empor. Allerlei seltsames Geräte stand umher. Ach Gott! - wie sich nun mein alter Vater zum Feuer herabbückte, da sah er ganz anders aus. Ein gräßlicher krampfhafter Schmerz schien seine sanften ehrlichen Züge zum häßlichen widerwärtigen Teufelsbilde verzogen zu haben. Er sah dem Coppelius ähnlich. Dieser schwang die glutrote Zange und holte damit hellblinkende Massen aus dem dicken Qualm, die er dann emsig häm-merte. Mir war es als würden Menschengesichter ringsumher sichtbar, aber ohne Augen - scheußliche, tiefe schwarze Höhlen statt ihrer. »Augen her, Augen her!« rief Coppelius mit dumpfer dröhnender Stimme. Ich kreischte auf von wildem Entsetzen gewaltig erfaßt und stürzte aus meinem Versteck heraus auf den Boden. Da ergriff mich Coppelius, »kleine Bestie! - kleine Bestie!« meckerte er zähnfletschend! - riß mich auf und warf mich auf den Herd, daß die Flamme mein Haar zu sengen begann: »Nun haben wir Augen - Augen - ein schön Paar Kinderaugen.« So flüsterte Coppelius, und griff mit den Fäusten glutrote Körner aus der Flamme, die er mir in die Augen streuen wollte. Da hob mein Vater flehend die Hände empor und rief. »Meister! Meister! laß meinem Nathanael die Augen - laß sie ihm!« Coppelius lachte gellend auf und rief. »Mag denn der Junge die Augen behalten und sein Pensum flennen in der Welt; aber nun wollen wir doch den Mechanismus der Hände und der Füße recht ob-servieren.« Und damit faßte er mich gewaltig, daß die Gelenke knackten, und schrob mir die Hände ab und die Füße und setzte sie bald hier, bald dort wieder ein. »'s steht doch überall nicht recht! 's gut so wie es war! - Der Alte hat's verstanden!« So zischte und lispelte Coppelius; aber alles um mich her wurde schwarz und finster, ein jäher Krampf durchzuckte Nerv und Gebein - ich fühlte nichts mehr.

I felt a soft warm breath fanning my cheek; I awakened as if out of the sleep of death; my mother was bending over me. "Is the Sandman still there?" I stammered. "No, my dear child; he's been gone a long, long time; he'll not hurt you." Thus spoke my mother, as she kissed her recovered darling and pressed him to her heart. But why should I tire you, my dear Lothair? why do I dwell at such length on these details, when there's so much remains to be said? Enough—I was detected in my eavesdropping, and roughly handled by Coppelius. Fear and terror had brought on a violent fever, of which I lay ill several weeks. "Is the Sandman still there?" these were the first words I uttered on coming to myself again, the first sign of my recovery, of my safety. Thus, you see, I have only to relate to you the most terrible moment of my youth for you to thoroughly understand that it must not be ascribed to the weakness of my eyesight if all that I see is colourless, but to the fact that a mysterious destiny has hung a dark veil of clouds about my life, which I shall perhaps only break through when I die.

Coppelius did not show himself again; it was reported he had left the town.

It was about a year later when, in pursuance of the old unchanged custom, we sat around the round table in the evening. Father was in very good spirits, and was telling us amusing tales about his youthful travels. As it was striking nine we all at once heard the street door creak on its hinges, and slow ponderous steps echoed across the passage and up the stairs. "That is Coppelius," said my mother, turning pale. "Yes, it is Coppelius," replied my father in a faint broken voice. The tears started from my mother's eyes. "But, father, father," she cried, "must it be so?" "This is the last time," he replied; "this is the last time he will come to me, I promise you. Go now, go and take the children. Go, go to bed—good-night."

As for me, I felt as if I were converted into cold, heavy stone; I could not get my breath. As I stood there immovable my mother seized me by the arm. "Come, Nathanael! do come along!" I suffered myself to be led away; I went into my room. "Be a good boy and keep quiet," mother called after me; "get into bed and go to sleep." But, tortured by indescribable fear and uneasiness, I could not close my eyes. That hateful, hideous Coppelius stood before me with his glittering eyes, smiling maliciously down upon me; in vain did I strive to banish the image. Somewhere about midnight there was a terrific crack, as if a cannon were being fired off. The whole house shook; something went rustling and clattering past my door; the house-door was pulled to with a bang. "That is Coppelius," I cried, terror-struck, and leapt out of bed. Then I heard a wild heartrending scream; I rushed into my father's room; the door stood open, and clouds of suffocating smoke came rolling towards me. The servant-maid shouted, "Oh! my master! my master!" On the floor in front of the smoking hearth lay my father, dead, his face burned black and fearfully distorted, my sisters weeping and moaning around him, and my mother lying near them in a swoon. "Coppelius, you atrocious fiend, you've killed my father," I shouted. My senses left me.

Ein sanfter warmer Hauch glitt über mein Gesicht, ich erwachte wie aus dem Todesschlaf, die Mutter hatte sich über mich hingebeugt. »Ist der Sandmann noch da?« stammelte ich. »Nein, mein liebes Kind, der ist lange, lange fort, der tut dir keinen Schaden!« - So sprach die Mutter und küßte und herzte den wiedergewonnenen Liebling.

Was soll ich Dich ermüden, mein herzlieber Lothar! was soll ich so weitläufig einzelnes hererzählen, da noch so vieles zu sagen übrig bleibt? Genug! - ich war bei der Lauscherei entdeckt, und von Coppelius gemißhandelt worden. Angst und Schrecken hatten mir ein hitziges Fieber zugezogen, an dem ich mehrere Wochen krank lag. »Ist der Sandmann noch da?« - Das war mein erstes gesundes Wort und das Zeichen meiner Genesung, meiner Rettung. - Nur noch den schrecklichsten Moment meiner Jugendjahre darf ich Dir erzählen; dann wirst Du überzeugt sein, daß es nicht meiner Augen Blödigkeit ist, wenn mir nun alles farblos erscheint, sondern, daß ein dunkles Verhängnis wirklich einen trüben Wolkenschleier über mein Leben gehängt hat, den ich vielleicht nur sterbend zerreiße.

Coppelius ließ sich nicht mehr sehen, es hieß, er habe die Stadt verlassen.

Ein Jahr mochte vergangen sein, als wir der alten unveränderten Sitte gemäß abends an dem runden Tische saßen. Der Vater war sehr heiter und erzählte viel Ergötzliches von den Reisen, die er in seiner Jugend gemacht. Da hörten wir, als es neune schlug, plötzlich die Haustür in den Angeln knarren und langsame eisenschwere Schritte dröhnten durch den Hausflur die Treppe herauf. »Das ist Coppelius«, sagte meine Mutter erblassend. »Ja! - es ist Coppelius«, wiederholte der Vater mit matter gebrochener Stimme. Die Tränen stürzten der Mutter aus den Augen. »Aber Vater, Vater!« rief sie, »muß es denn so sein?« - »Zum letzten Male!« erwiderte dieser, »zum letzten Male kommt er zu mir, ich verspreche es dir. Geh nur, geh mit den Kindern! - Geht - geht zu Bette! Gute Nacht!«

Mir war es, als sei ich in schweren kalten Stein eingepreßt - mein Atem stockte! - Die Mutter ergriff mich beim Arm als ich unbeweglich stehen blieb: »Komm Nathanael, komme nur!« Ich ließ mich fortführen, ich trat in meine Kammer. »Sei ruhig, sei ruhig, lege dich ins Bette! - schlafe - schlafe«, rief mir die Mutter nach; aber von unbeschreiblicher innerer Angst und Unruhe gequält, konnte ich kein Auge zutun. Der verhaßte abscheuliche Coppelius stand vor mir mit funkelnden Augen und lachte mich hämisch an, vergebens trachtete ich sein Bild los zu werden. Es mochte wohl schon Mitternacht sein, als ein entsetzlicher Schlag geschah, wie wenn ein Geschütz losgefeuert würde. Das ganze Haus erdröhnte, es rasselte und rauschte bei meiner Türe vorüber, die Haustüre wurde klirrend zugeworfen. »Das ist Coppelius!« rief ich entsetzt und sprang aus dem Bette. Da kreischte es auf in schneidendem trostlosen Jammer, fort stürzte ich nach des Vaters Zimmer, die Türe stand offen, erstickender Dampf quoll mir entgegen, das Dienstmädchen schrie: »Ach, der Herr! - der Herr!« - Vor dem dampfenden Herde auf dem Boden lag mein Vater tot mit schwarz verbranntem gräßlich verzerrtem Gesicht, um ihn herum heulten und winselten die Schwestern - die Mutter ohnmächtig daneben! - »Coppelius, verruchter Satan, du hast den Vater erschlagen!« - So schrie ich auf, mir vergingen die Sinne.

Two days later, when my father was placed in his coffin, his features were mild and gentle again as they had been when he was alive. I found great consolation in the thought that his association with the diabolical Coppelius could not have ended in his everlasting ruin.

Our neighbours had been awakened by the explosion; the affair got talked about, and came before the magisterial authorities, who wished to cite Coppelius to clear himself. But he had disappeared from the place, leaving no traces behind him.

Now when I tell you, my dear friend, that the weather-glass hawker I spoke of was the villain Coppelius, you will not blame me for seeing impending mischief in his inauspicious reappearance. He was differently dressed; but Coppelius's figure and features are too deeply impressed upon my mind for me to be capable of making a mistake in the matter. Moreover, he has not even changed his name. He proclaims himself here, I learn, to be a Piedmontese mechanician, and styles himself Giuseppe Coppola.

I am resolved to enter the lists against him and revenge my father's death, let the consequences be what they may.

Don't say a word to mother about the reappearance of this odious monster. Give my love to my darling Clara; I will write to her when I am in a somewhat calmer frame of mind.

                                                                              Adieu, &c.

Als man zwei Tage darauf meinen Vater in den Sarg legte, waren seine Gesichtszüge wieder mild und sanft geworden, wie sie im Leben waren. Tröstend ging es in meiner Seele auf, daß sein Bund mit dem teuflischen Coppelius ihn nicht ins ewige Verderben gestürzt haben könne.

Die Explosion hatte die Nachbarn geweckt, der Vorfall wurde ruchtbar und kam vor die Obrigkeit, welche den Coppelius zur Verantwortung vorfordern wollte. Der war aber spurlos vom Orte verschwunden.

Wenn ich Dir nun sage, mein herzlieber Freund! daß jener Wetterglashändler eben der verruchte Coppelius war, so wirst Du mir es nicht verargen, daß ich die feindliche Erscheinung als schweres Unheil bringend deute. Er war anders gekleidet, aber Coppelius' Figur und Gesichtszüge sind zu tief in mein Innerstes eingeprägt, als daß hier ein Irrtum möglich sein sollte. Zudem hat Coppelius nicht einmal seinen Namen geändert. Er gibt sich hier, wie ich höre, für einen piemontesischen Mechanikus aus, und nennt sich Giuseppe Coppola.

Ich bin entschlossen es mit ihm aufzunehmen und des Vaters Tod zu rächen, mag es denn nun gehen wie es will.

Der Mutter erzähle nichts von dem Erscheinen des gräßlichen Unholds
- Grüße meine liebe holde Clara, ich schreibe ihr in ruhigerer Gemütsstimmung.

Lebe wohl etc. etc.

E.T.A. Hoffmann (1776-1822)

The Conscience by François Chifflart (1877)

CLARA TO NATHANAEL

You are right, you have not written to me for a very long time, but nevertheless I believe that I still retain a place in your mind and thoughts. It is a proof
that you were thinking a good deal about me when you were sending off your
last letter to brother Lothair, for instead of directing it to him you directed it to
me. With joy I tore open the envelope, and did not perceive the mistake until I
read the words, "Oh! my dear, dear Lothair." Now I know I ought not to have
read any more of the letter, but ought to have given it to my brother. But as you
have so often in innocent raillery made it a sort of reproach against me that I
possessed such a calm, and, for a woman, cool-headed temperament that I
should be like the woman we read of—if the house was threatening to tumble
down, I should, before hastily fleeing, stop to smooth down a crumple in the
window-curtains—I need hardly tell you that the beginning of your letter quite
upset me. I could scarcely breathe; there was a bright mist before my eyes. Oh!
my darling Nathanael! what could this terrible thing be that had happened?
Separation from you—never to see you again, the thought was like a sharp knife
in my heart. I read on and on. Your description of that horrid Coppelius made
my flesh creep. I now learnt for the first time what a terrible and violent death
your good old father died. Brother Lothair, to whom I handed over his property, sought to comfort me, but with little success. That horrid weather-glass
hawker Giuseppe Coppola followed me everywhere; and I am almost ashamed
to confess it, but he was able to disturb my sound and in general calm sleep
with all sorts of wonderful dream-shapes. But soon—the next day—I saw
everything in a different light. Oh! do not be angry with me, my best-beloved, if,
despite your strange presentiment that Coppelius will do you some mischief,
Lothair tells you I am in quite as good spirits, and just the same as ever.

I will frankly confess, it seems to me that all that was fearsome and terrible
of which you speak, existed only in your own self, and that the real true outer
world had but little to do with it. I can quite admit that old Coppelius may have
been highly obnoxious to you children, but your real detestation of him arose
from the fact that he hated children.

Clara an Nathanael

Wahr ist es, daß Du recht lange mir nicht geschrieben hast, aber dennoch glaube ich, daß Du mich in Sinn und Gedanken trägst. Denn meiner gedachtest Du wohl recht lebhaft, als Du Deinen letzten Brief an Bruder Lothar absenden wolltest und die Aufschrift, statt an ihn an mich richtetest. Freudig erbrach ich den Brief und wurde den Irrtum erst bei den Worten inne: »Ach mein herzlieber Lothar!« - Nun hätte ich nicht weiter lesen, sondern den Brief dem Bruder geben sollen. Aber, hast Du mir auch sonst manchmal in kindischer Neckerei vorgeworfen, ich hätte solch ruhiges, weiblich besonnenes Gemüt, daß ich wie jene Frau, drohe das Haus den Einsturz, noch vor schneller Flucht ganz geschwinde einen falschen Kniff in der Fenstergardine glattstreichen würde, so darf ich doch wohl kaum versichern, daß Deines Briefes Anfang mich tief erschütterte. Ich konnte kaum atmen, es flimmerte mir vor den Augen. - Ach, mein herzgeliebter Nathanael! was konnte so Entsetzliches in Dein Leben getreten sein! Trennung von Dir, Dich niemals wiedersehen, der Gedanke durchfuhr meine Brust wie ein glühender Dolchstich. - Ich las und las! - Deine Schilderung des widerwärtigen Coppelius ist gräßlich. Erst jetzt vernahm ich, wie Dein guter alter Vater solch entsetzlichen, gewaltsamen Todes starb. Bruder Lothar, dem ich sein Eigentum zustellte, suchte mich zu beruhigen, aber es gelang ihm schlecht. Der fatale Wetterglashändler Giuseppe Coppola verfolgte mich auf Schritt und Tritt und beinahe schäme ich mich, es zu gestehen, daß er selbst meinen gesunden, sonst so ruhigen Schlaf in allerlei wunderlichen Traumgebilden zerstören konnte. Doch bald, schon den andern Tag, hatte sich alles anders in mir gestaltet. Sei mir nur nicht böse, mein Inniggeliebter, wenn Lothar Dir etwa sagen möchte, daß ich trotz Deiner seltsamen Ahnung, Coppelius werde Dir etwas Böses antun, ganz heitern unbefangenen Sinnes bin, wie immer.

Geradeheraus will ich es Dir nur gestehen, daß, wie ich meine, alles Entsetzliche und Schreckliche, wovon Du sprichst, nur in Deinem Innern vorging, die wahre wirkliche Außenwelt aber daran wohl wenig teilhatte. Widerwärtig genug mag der alte Coppelius gewesen sein, aber daß er Kinder haßte, das brachte in Euch Kindern wahren Abscheu gegen ihn hervor.

Naturally enough the gruesome Sandman of the old nurse's story was associated in your childish mind with old Coppelius, who, even though you had not believed in the Sandman, would have been to you a ghostly bugbear, especially dangerous to children. His mysterious labours along with your father at night-time were, I daresay, nothing more than secret experiments in alchemy, with which your mother could not be over well pleased, owing to the large sums of money that most likely were thrown away upon them; and besides, your father, his mind full of the deceptive striving after higher knowledge, may probably have become rather indifferent to his family, as so often happens in the case of such experimentalists. So also it is equally probable that your father brought about his death by his own imprudence, and that Coppelius is not to blame for it. I must tell you that yesterday I asked our experienced neighbour, the chemist, whether in experiments of this kind an explosion could take place which would have a momentarily fatal effect. He said, "Oh, certainly!" and described to me in his prolix and circumstantial way how it could be occasioned, mentioning at the same time so many strange and funny words that I could not remember them at all. Now I know you will be angry at your Clara, and will say, "Of the Mysterious which often clasps man in its invisible arms there's not a ray can find its way into this cold heart. She sees only the varied surface of the things of the world, and, like the little child, is pleased with the golden glittering fruit; at the kernel of which lies the fatal poison."

Oh! my beloved Nathanael, do you believe then that the intuitive prescience of a dark power working within us to our own ruin cannot exist also in minds which are cheerful, natural, free from care? But please forgive me that I, a simple girl, presume in any way to indicate to you what I really think of such an inward strife. After all, I should not find the proper words, and you would only laugh at me, not because my thoughts were stupid, but because I was so foolish as to attempt to tell them to you.

Natürlich verknüpfte sich nun in Deinem kindischen Gemüt der schreckliche Sandmann aus dem Ammenmärchen mit dem alten Coppelius, der Dir, glaubtest Du auch nicht an den Sandmann, ein gespenstischer, Kindern vorzüglich gefährlicher, Unhold blieb. Das unheimliche Treiben mit Deinem Vater zur Nachtzeit war wohl nichts anders, als daß beide insgeheim alchymistische Versuche machten, womit die Mutter nicht zufrieden sein konnte, da gewiß viel Geld unnütz verschleudert und obendrein, wie es immer mit solchen Laboranten der Fall sein soll, des Vaters Gemüt ganz von dem trügerischen Drange nach hoher Weisheit erfüllt, der Familie abwendig gemacht wurde. Der Vater hat wohl gewiß durch eigne Unvorsichtigkeit seinen Tod herbeigeführt, und Coppelius ist nicht schuld daran: Glaubst Du, daß ich den erfahrnen Nachbar Apotheker gestern frug, ob wohl bei chemischen Versuchen eine solche augenblicklich tötende Explosion möglich sei? Der sagte: »Ei allerdings« und beschrieb mir nach seiner Art gar weitläufig und umständlich, wie das zugehen könne, und nannte dabei so viel sonderbar klingende Namen, die ich gar nicht zu behalten vermochte. - Nun wirst Du wohl unwillig werden über Deine Clara, Du wirst sagen: »In dies kalte Gemüt dringt kein Strahl des Geheimnisvollen, das den Menschen oft mit unsichtbaren Armen umfaßt; sie erschaut nur die bunte Oberfläche der Welt und freut sich, wie das kindische Kind über die goldgleißende Frucht, in deren Innern tödliches Gift verborgen.«

Ach mein herzgeliebter Nathanael! glaubst Du denn nicht, daß auch in heitern - unbefangenen - sorglosen Gemütern die Ahnung wohnen könne von einer dunklen Macht, die feindlich uns in unserm eignen Selbst zu verderben strebt? - Aber verzeih es mir, wenn ich einfältig Mädchen mich unterfange, auf irgend eine Weise Dir anzudeuten, was ich eigentlich von solchem Kampfe im Innern glaube. - Ich finde wohl gar am Ende nicht die rechten Worte und Du lachst mich aus, nicht, weil ich was Dummes meine, sondern weil ich mich so ungeschickt anstelle, es zu sagen.

If there is a dark and hostile power which traitorously fixes a thread in our hearts in order that, laying hold of it and drawing us by means of it along a dangerous road to ruin, which otherwise we should not have trod—if, I say, there is such a power, it must assume within us a form like ourselves, nay, it must be ourselves; for only in that way can we believe in it, and only so understood do we yield to it so far that it is able to accomplish its secret purpose. So long as we have sufficient firmness, fortified by cheerfulness, to always acknowledge foreign hostile influences for what they really are, whilst we quietly pursue the path pointed out to us by both inclination and calling, then this mysterious power perishes in its futile struggles to attain the form which is to be the reflected image of ourselves. It is also certain, Lothair adds, that if we have once voluntarily given ourselves up to this dark physical power, it often reproduces within us the strange forms which the outer world throws in our way, so that thus it is we ourselves who engender within ourselves the spirit which by some remarkable delusion we imagine to speak in that outer form. It is the phantom of our own self whose intimate relationship with, and whose powerful influence upon our soul either plunges us into hell or elevates us to heaven. Thus you will see, my beloved Nathanael, that I and brother Lothair have well talked over the subject of dark powers and forces; and now, after I have with some difficulty written down the principal results of our discussion, they seem to me to contain many really profound thoughts. Lothair's last words, however, I don't quite understand altogether; I only dimly guess what he means; and yet I cannot help thinking it is all very true, I beg you, dear, strive to forget the ugly advocate Coppelius as well as the weather-glass hawker Giuseppe Coppola. Try and convince yourself that these foreign influences can have no power over you, that it is only the belief in their hostile power which can in reality make them dangerous to you. If every line of your letter did not betray the violent excitement of your mind, and if I did not sympathise with your condition from the bottom of my heart, I could in truth jest about the advocate Sandman and weather-glass hawker Coppelius. Pluck up your spirits! Be cheerful! I have resolved to appear to you as your guardian-angel if that ugly man Coppola should dare take it into his head to bother you in your dreams, and drive him away with a good hearty laugh. I'm not afraid of him and his nasty hands, not the least little bit; I won't let him either as advocate spoil any dainty tit-bit I've taken, or as Sandman rob me of my eyes.

My darling, darling Nathanael,
Eternally your, &c. &c.

Gibt es eine dunkle Macht, die so recht feindlich und verräterisch einen Faden in unser Inneres legt, woran sie uns dann festpackt und fortzieht auf einem gefahrvollen verderblichen Wege, den wir sonst nicht betreten haben würden - gibt es eine solche Macht, so muß sie in uns sich, wie wir selbst gestalten, ja unser Selbst werden; denn nur so glauben wir an sie und räumen ihr den Platz ein, dessen sie bedarf, um jenes geheime Werk zu vollbringen. Haben wir festen, durch das heitre Leben gestärkten, Sinn genug, um fremdes feindliches Einwirken als solches stets zu erkennen und den Weg, in den uns Neigung und Beruf geschoben, ruhigen Schrittes zu verfolgen, so geht wohl jene unheimliche Macht unter in dem vergeblichen Ringen nach der Gestaltung, die unser eignes Spiegelbild sein sollte. Es ist auch gewiß, fügt Lothar hinzu, daß die dunkle psychische Macht, haben wir uns durch uns selbst ihr hingegeben, oft fremde Gestalten, die die Außenwelt uns in den Weg wirft, in unser Inneres hineinzieht, so, daß wir selbst nur den Geist entzünden, der, wie wir in wunderlicher Täuschung glauben, aus jener Gestalt spricht. Es ist das Phantom unseres eigenen Ichs, dessen innige Verwandtschaft und dessen tiefe Einwirkung auf unser Gemüt uns in die Hölle wirft, oder in den Himmel verzückt. - Du merkst, mein herzlieber Nathanael! daß wir, ich und Bruder Lothar uns recht über die Materie von dunklen Mächten und Gewalten ausgesprochen haben, die mir nun, nachdem ich nicht ohne Mühe das Hauptsächlichste aufgeschrieben, ordentlich tiefsinnig vorkommt. Lothars letzte Worte verstehe ich nicht ganz, ich ahne nur, was er meint, und doch ist es mir, als sei alles sehr wahr. Ich bitte Dich, schlage Dir den häßlichen Advokaten Coppelius und den Wetterglasmann Giuseppe Coppola ganz aus dem Sinn. Sei überzeugt, daß diese fremden Gestalten nichts über Dich vermögen; nur der Glaube an ihre feindliche Gewalt kann sie Dir in der Tat feindlich machen. Spräche nicht aus jeder Zeile Deines Briefes die tiefste Aufregung Deines Gemüts, schmerzte mich nicht Dein Zustand recht in innerster Seele, wahrhaftig, ich könnte über den Advokaten Sandmann und den Wetterglashändler Coppelius scherzen. Sei heiter - heiter! - Ich habe mir vorgenommen, bei Dir zu erscheinen, wie Dein Schutzgeist, und den häßlichen Coppola, sollte er es sich etwa beikommen lassen, Dir im Traum beschwerlich zu fallen, mit lautem Lachen fortzubannen. Ganz und gar nicht fürchte ich mich vor ihm und vor seinen garstigen Fäusten, er soll mir weder als Advokat eine Näscherei, noch als Sandmann die Augen verderben.

Ewig, mein herzinnigstgeliebter Nathanael etc. etc. etc.

NATHANAEL TO LOTHAIR

I am very sorry that Clara opened and read my last letter to you; of course the mistake is to be attributed to my own absence of mind. She has written me a very deep philosophical letter, proving conclusively that Coppelius and Coppola only exist in my own mind and are phantoms of my own self, which will at once be dissipated, as soon as I look upon them in that light. In very truth one can hardly believe that the mind which so often sparkles in those bright, beautifully smiling, childlike eyes of hers like a sweet lovely dream could draw such subtle and scholastic distinctions. She also mentions your name. You have been talking about me. I suppose you have been giving her lectures, since she sifts and refines everything so acutely. But enough of this! I must now tell you it is most certain that the weather-glass hawker Giuseppe Coppola is not the advocate Coppelius. I am attending the lectures of our recently appointed Professor of Physics, who, like the distinguished naturalist, is called Spalanzani, and is of Italian origin. He has known Coppola for many years; and it is also easy to tell from his accent that he really is a Piedmontese. Coppelius was a German, though no honest German, I fancy. Nevertheless I am not quite satisfied. You and Clara will perhaps take me for a gloomy dreamer, but nohow can I get rid of the impression which Coppelius's cursed face made upon me. I am glad to learn from Spalanzani that he has left the town. This Professor Spalanzani is a very queer fish. He is a little fat man, with prominent cheek-bones, thin nose, projecting lips, and small piercing eyes. You cannot get a better picture of him than by turning over one of the Berlin pocket-almanacs and looking at Cagliostro's portrait engraved by Chodowiecki; Spalanzani looks just like him.

Nathanael an Lothar

Sehr unlieb ist es mir, daß Clara neulich den Brief an Dich aus, freilich durch meine Zerstreutheit veranlagtem, Irrtum erbrach und las. Sie hat mir einen sehr tiefsinnigen philosophischen Brief geschrieben, worin sie ausführlich beweiset, daß Coppelius und Coppola nur in meinem Innern existieren und Phantome meines Ichs sind, die augenblicklich zerstäuben, wenn ich sie als solche erkenne. In der Tat, man sollte gar nicht glauben, daß der Geist, der aus solch hellen holdlächelnden Kindesaugen, oft wie ein lieblicher süßer Traum, hervorleuchtet, so gar verständig, so magistermäßig distinguieren könne. Sie beruft sich auf Dich. Ihr habt über mich gesprochen. Du liesest ihr wohl logische Kollegia, damit sie alles fein sichten und sondern lerne. - Laß das bleiben! - Übrigens ist es wohl gewiß, daß der Wetterglashändler Giuseppe Coppola keinesweges der alte Advokat Coppelius ist. Ich höre bei dem erst neuerdings angekommenen Professor der Physik, der, wie jener berühmte Naturforscher, Spalanzani heißt und italienischer Abkunft ist, Kollegia. Der kennt den Coppola schon seit vielen Jahren und überdem hört man es auch seiner Aussprache an, daß er wirklich Piemonteser ist. Coppelius war ein Deutscher, aber wie mich dünkt, kein ehrlicher. Ganz beruhigt bin ich nicht. Haltet Ihr, Du und Clara, mich immerhin für einen düstern Träumer, aber nicht los kann ich den Eindruck werden, den Coppelius' verfluchtes Gesicht auf mich macht. Ich bin froh, daß er fort ist aus der Stadt, wie mir Spalanzani sagt. Dieser Professor ist ein wunderlicher Kauz. Ein kleiner rundlicher Mann, das Gesicht mit starken Backenknochen, feiner Nase, aufgeworfenen Lippen, kleinen stechenden Augen. Doch besser, als in jeder Beschreibung, siehst Du ihn, wenn Du den Cagliostro, wie er von Chodowiecki in irgend einem Berlinischen Taschenkalender steht, anschauest. - So sieht Spalanzani aus.

Once lately, as I went up the steps to his house, I perceived that beside the curtain which generally covered a glass door there was a small chink. What it was that excited my curiosity I cannot explain; but I looked through. In the room I saw a female, tall, very slender, but of perfect proportions, and splendidly dressed, sitting at a little table, on which she had placed both her arms, her hands being folded together. She sat opposite the door, so that I could easily see her angelically beautiful face. She did not appear to notice me, and there was moreover a strangely fixed look about her eyes, I might almost say they appeared as if they had no power of vision; I thought she was sleeping with her eyes open. I felt quite uncomfortable, and so I slipped away quietly into the Professor's lecture-room, which was close at hand. Afterwards I learnt that the figure which I had seen was Spalanzani's daughter, Olimpia, whom he keeps locked in a most wicked and unaccountable way, and no man is ever allowed to come near her. Perhaps, however, there is after all, something peculiar about her; perhaps she's an idiot or something of that sort. But why am I telling you all this? I could have told you it all better and more in detail when I see you. For in a fortnight I shall be amongst you. I must see my dear sweet angel, my Clara, again. Then the little bit of ill-temper, which, I must confess, took possession of me after her fearfully sensible letter, will be blown away. And that is the reason why I am not writing to her as well today.

                                                            With all best wishes, &c.

Neulich steige ich die Treppe herauf und nehme wahr, daß die sonst einer Glastüre dicht vorgezogene Gardine zur Seite einen kleinen Spalt läßt. Selbst weiß ich nicht, wie ich dazu kam, neugierig durchzublicken. Ein hohes, sehr schlank im reinsten Ebenmaß gewachsenes, herrlich gekleidetes Frauenzimmer saß im Zimmer vor einem kleinen Tisch, auf den sie beide Ärme, die Hände zusammengefaltet, gelegt hatte. Sie saß der Türe gegenüber, so, daß ich ihr engelschönes Gesicht ganz erblickte. Sie schien mich nicht zu bemerken, und überhaupt hatten ihre Augen etwas Starres, beinahe möcht ich sagen, keine Sehkraft, es war mir so, als schliefe sie mit offnen Augen. Mir wurde ganz unheimlich und deshalb schlich ich leise fort ins Auditorium, das daneben gelegen. Nachher erfuhr ich, daß die Gestalt, die ich gesehen, Spalanzanis Tochter, Olimpia war, die er sonderbarer und schlechter Weise einsperrt, so, daß durchaus kein Mensch in ihre Nähe kommen darf. - Am Ende hat es eine Bewandtnis mit ihr, sie ist vielleicht blödsinnig oder sonst. - Weshalb schreibe ich Dir aber das alles? Besser und ausführlicher hätte ich Dir das mündlich erzählen können. Wisse nämlich, daß ich über vierzehn Tage bei Euch bin. Ich muß mein süßes liebes Engelsbild, meine Clara, wiedersehen. Weggehaucht wird dann die Verstimmung sein, die sich (ich muß das gestehen) nach dem fatalen verständigen Briefe meiner bemeistern wollte. Deshalb schreibe ich auch heute nicht an sie.

Tausend Grüße etc. etc. etc.

Recovering my courage with an effort, I take a cautious peep out

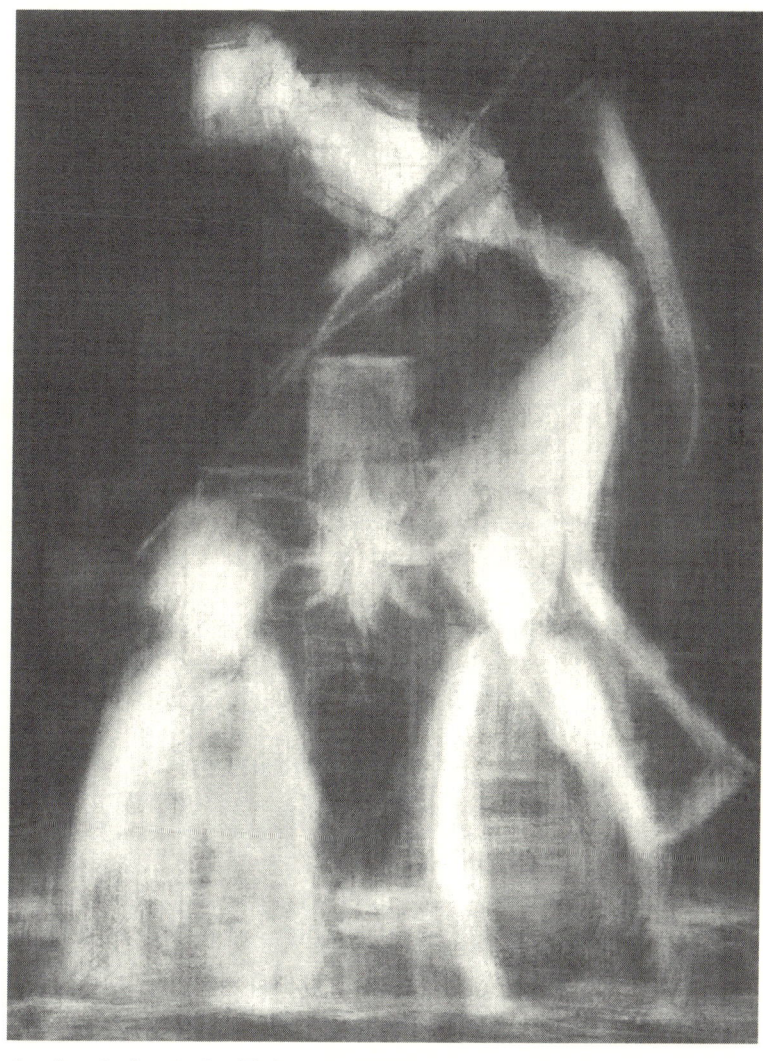

Death, where is thy sting?—Tod, wo ist dein Stachel? by Christian Rohlfs (c. 1900)

Nothing more strange and extraordinary can be imagined, gracious reader, than what happened to my poor friend, the young student Nathanael, and which I have undertaken to relate to you. Have you ever lived to experience anything that completely took possession of your heart and mind and thoughts to the utter exclusion of everything else? All was seething and boiling within you; your blood, heated to fever pitch, leapt through your veins and inflamed your cheeks. Your gaze was so peculiar, as if seeking to grasp in empty space forms not seen of any other eye, and all your words ended in sighs betokening some mystery. Then your friends asked you, "What is the matter with you, my dear friend? What do you see?" And, wishing to describe the inner pictures in all their vivid colours, with their lights and their shades, you in vain struggled to find words with which to express yourself. But you felt as if you must gather up all the events that had happened, wonderful, splendid, terrible, jocose, and awful, in the very first word, so that the whole might be revealed by a single electric discharge, so to speak. Yet every word and all that partook of the nature of communication by intelligible sounds seemed to be colourless, cold, and dead. Then you try and try again, and stutter and stammer, whilst your friends' prosy questions strike like icy winds upon your heart's hot fire until they extinguish it. But if, like a bold painter, you had first sketched in a few audacious strokes the outline of the picture you had in your soul, you would then easily have been able to deepen and intensify the colours one after the other, until the varied throng of living figures carried your friends away, and they, like you, saw themselves in the midst of the scene that had proceeded out of your own soul.

Strictly speaking, indulgent reader, I must indeed confess to you, nobody has asked me for the history of young Nathanael; but you are very well aware that I belong to that remarkable class of authors who, when they are bearing anything about in their minds in the manner I have just described, feel as if everybody who comes near them, and also the whole world to boot, were asking, "Oh! what is it? Oh! do tell us, my good sir?" Hence I was most powerfully impelled to narrate to you Nathanael's ominous life. My soul was full of the elements of wonder and extraordinary peculiarity in it; but, for this very reason, and because it was necessary in the very beginning to dispose you, indulgent reader, to bear with what is fantastic—and that is not a little thing—I racked my brain to find a way of commencing the story in a significant and original manner, calculated to arrest your attention.

Seltsamer und wunderlicher kann nichts erfunden werden, als dasjenige ist, was sich mit meinem armen Freunde, dem jungen Studenten Nathanael, zugetragen, und was ich dir, günstiger Leser! zu erzählen unternommen. Hast du, Geneigtester! wohl jemals etwas erlebt, das deine Brust, Sinn und Gedanken ganz und gar erfüllte, alles andere daraus verdrängend? Es gärte und kochte in dir, zur siedenden Glut entzündet sprang das Blut durch die Adern und färbte höher deine Wangen. Dein Blick war so seltsam als wolle er Gestalten, keinem andern Auge sichtbar, im leeren Raum erfassen und die Rede zerfloß in dunkle Seufzer. Da frugen dich die Freunde: »Wie ist Ihnen, Verehrter? - Was haben Sie, Teurer?« Und nun wolltest du das innere Gebilde mit allen glühenden Farben und Schatten und Lichtern aussprechen und mühtest dich ab, Worte zu finden, um nur anzufangen. Aber es war dir, als müßtest du nun gleich im ersten Wort alles Wunderbare, Herrliche, Entsetzliche, Lustige, Grauenhafte, das sich zugetragen, recht zusammengreifen, so daß es, wie ein elektrischer Schlag, alle treffe. Doch jedes Wort, alles was Rede vermag, schien dir farblos und frostig und tot. Du suchst und suchst, und stotterst und stammelst, und die nüchternen Fragen der Freunde schlagen, wie eisige Windeshauche, hinein in deine innere Glut, bis sie verlöschen will. Hattest du aber, wie ein kecker Maler, erst mit einigen verwegenen Strichen, den Umriß deines innern Bildes hingeworfen, so trugst du mit leichter Mühe immer glühender und glühender die Farben auf und das lebendige Gewühl mannigfacher Gestalten riß die Freunde fort und sie sahen, wie du, sich selbst mitten im Bilde, das aus deinem Gemüt hervorgegangen! - Mich hat, wie ich es dir, geneigter Leser! gestehen muß, eigentlich niemand nach der Geschichte des jungen Nathanael gefragt; du weißt ja aber wohl, daß ich zu dem wunderlichen Geschlechte der Autoren gehöre, denen, tragen sie etwas so in sich, wie ich es vorhin beschrieben, so zumute wird, als frage jeder, der in ihre Nähe kommt und nebenher auch wohl noch die ganze Welt: »Was ist es denn? Erzählen Sie Liebster?« - So trieb es mich denn gar gewaltig, von Nathanaels verhängnisvollem Leben zu dir zu sprechen. Das Wunderbare, Seltsame davon erfüllte meine ganze Seele, aber eben deshalb und weil ich dich, o mein Leser! gleich geneigt machen mußte, Wunderliches zu ertragen, welches nichts Geringes ist, quälte ich mich ab, Nathanaels Geschichte, bedeutend - originell, ergreifend, anzufangen:

To begin with "Once upon a time," the best beginning for a story, seemed to me too tame; with "In the small country town S—— lived," rather better, at any rate allowing plenty of room to work up to the climax; or to plunge at once in medias res, "'Go to the devil!' cried the student Nathanael, his eyes blazing wildly with rage and fear, when the weather-glass hawker Giuseppe Coppola"—well, that is what I really had written, when I thought I detected something of the ridiculous in Nathanael's wild glance; and the history is anything but laughable. I could not find any words which seemed fitted to reflect in even the feeblest degree the brightness of the colours of my mental vision. I determined not to begin at all. So I pray you, gracious reader, accept the three letters which my friend Lothair has been so kind as to communicate to me as the outline of the picture, into which I will endeavour to introduce more and more colour as I proceed with my narrative. Perhaps, like a good portrait-painter, I may succeed in depicting more than one figure in such wise that you will recognise it as a good likeness without being acquainted with the original, and feel as if you had very often seen the original with your own bodily eyes. Perhaps, too, you will then believe that nothing is more wonderful, nothing more fantastic than real life, and that all that a writer can do is to present it as a dark reflection from a dim cut mirror.

In order to make the very commencement more intelligible, it is necessary to add to the letters that, soon after the death of Nathanael's father, Clara and Lothair, the children of a distant relative, who had likewise died, leaving them orphans, were taken by Nathanael's mother into her own house. Clara and Nathanael conceived a warm affection for each other, against which not the slightest objection in the world could be urged. When therefore Nathanael left home to prosecute his studies in G——, they were betrothed. It is from G—— that his last letter is written, where he is attending the lectures of Spalanzani, the distinguished Professor of Physics.

»Es war einmal« - der schönste Anfang jeder Erzählung, zu nüchtern! - »In der kleinen Provinzialstadt S. lebte« - etwas besser, wenigstens ausholend zum Klimax. - Oder gleich medias in res: »>Scher er sich zum Teufel<, rief, Wut und Entsetzen im wilden Blick, der Student Nathanael, als der Wetterglashändler Giuseppe Coppola« - Das hatte ich in der Tat schon aufgeschrieben, als ich in dem wilden Blick des Studenten Nathanael etwas Possierliches zu verspüren glaubte; die Geschichte ist aber gar nicht spaßhaft. Mir kam keine Rede in den Sinn, die nur im mindesten etwas von dem Farbenglanz des innern Bildes abzuspiegeln schien. Ich beschloß gar nicht anzufangen. Nimm, geneigter Leser! die drei Briefe, welche Freund Lothar mir gütigst mitteilte, für den Umriß des Gebildes, in das ich nun erzählend immer mehr und mehr Farbe hineinzutragen mich bemühen werde. Vielleicht gelingt es mir, manche Gestalt, wie ein guter Porträtmaler, so aufzufassen, daß du es ähnlich findest, ohne das Original zu kennen, ja daß es dir ist, als hättest du die Person recht oft schon mit leibhaftigen Augen gesehen. Vielleicht wirst du, o mein Leser! dann glauben, daß nichts wunderlicher und toller sei, als das wirkliche Leben und daß dieses der Dichter doch nur, wie in eines matt geschliffnen Spiegels dunklem Widerschein, auffassen könne.

Damit klarer werde, was gleich anfangs zu wissen nötig, ist jenen Briefen noch hinzuzufügen, daß bald darauf, als Nathanaels Vater gestorben, Clara und Lothar, Kinder eines weitläuftigen Verwandten, der ebenfalls gestorben und sie verwaist nachgelassen, von Nathanaels Mutter ins Haus genommen wurden. Clara und Nathanael faßten eine heftige Zuneigung zueinander, wogegen kein Mensch auf Erden etwas einzuwenden hatte; sie waren daher Verlobte, als Nathanael den Ort verließ um seine Studien in G. - fortzusetzen. Da ist er nun in seinem letzten Brief und hört Kollegia bei dem berühmten Professor Physices, Spalanzani.

I might now proceed comfortably with my narration, did not at this moment Clara's image rise up so vividly before my eyes that I cannot turn them away from it, just as I never could when she looked upon me and smiled so sweetly. Nowhere would she have passed for beautiful; that was the unanimous opinion of all who professed to have any technical knowledge of beauty. But whilst architects praised the pure proportions of her figure and form, painters averred that her neck, shoulders, and bosom were almost too chastely modelled, and yet, on the other hand, one and all were in love with her glorious Magdalene hair, and talked a good deal of nonsense about Battoni-like colouring. One of them, a veritable romanticist, strangely enough likened her eyes to a lake by Ruisdael, in which is reflected the pure azure of the cloudless sky, the beauty of woods and flowers, and all the bright and varied life of a living landscape. Poets and musicians went still further and said, "What's all this talk about seas and reflections? How can we look upon the girl without feeling that wonderful heavenly songs and melodies beam upon us from her eyes, penetrating deep down into our hearts, till all becomes awake and throbbing with emotion? And if we cannot sing anything at all passable then, why, we are not worth much; and this we can also plainly read in the rare smile which flits around her lips when we have the hardihood to squeak out something in her presence which we pretend to call singing, in spite of the fact that it is nothing more than a few single notes confusedly linked together." And it really was so. Clara had the powerful fancy of a bright, innocent, unaffected child, a woman's deep and sympathetic heart, and an understanding clear, sharp, and discriminating. Dreamers and visionaries had but a bad time of it with her; for without saying very much—she was not by nature of a talkative disposition—she plainly asked, by her calm steady look, and rare ironical smile, "How can you imagine, my dear friends, that I can take these fleeting shadowy images for true living and breathing forms?" For this reason many found fault with her as being cold, prosaic, and devoid of feeling; others, however, who had reached a clearer and deeper conception of life, were extremely fond of the intelligent, childlike, large-hearted girl But none had such an affection for her as Nathanael, who was a zealous and cheerful cultivator of the fields of science and art. Clara clung to her lover with all her heart; the first clouds she encountered in life were when he had to separate from her. With what delight did she fly into his arms when, as he had promised in his last letter to Lothair, he really came back to his native town and entered his mother's room! And as Nathanael had foreseen, the moment he saw Clara again he no longer thought about either the advocate Coppelius or her sensible letter; his ill-humour had quite disappeared.

Nun könnte ich getrost in der Erzählung fortfahren; aber in dem Augenblick steht Claras Bild so lebendig mir vor Augen, daß ich nicht wegschauen kann, so wie es immer geschah, wenn sie mich holdlächelnd anblickte. - Für schön konnte Clara keinesweges gelten; das meinten alle, die sich von Amtswegen auf Schönheit verstehen. Doch lobten die Architekten die reinen Verhältnisse ihres Wuchses, die Maler fanden Nacken, Schultern und Brust beinahe zu keusch geformt, verliebten sich dagegen sämtlich in das wunderbare Magdalenenhaar und faselten überhaupt viel von Battonischem Kolorit. Einer von ihnen, ein wirklicher Fantast, verglich aber höchstseltsamer Weise Claras Augen mit einem See von Ruisdael, in dem sich des wolkenlosen Himmels reines Azur, Wald- und Blumenflur, der reichen Landschaft ganzes buntes, heitres Leben spiegelt. Dichter und Meister gingen aber weiter und sprachen: »Was See - was Spiegel! - Können wir denn das Mädchen anschauen, ohne daß uns aus ihrem Blick wunderbare himmlische Gesänge und Klänge entgegenstrahlen, die in unser Innerstes dringen, daß da alles wach und rege wird? Singen wir selbst dann nichts wahrhaft Gescheutes, so ist überhaupt nicht viel an uns und das lesen wir denn auch deutlich in dem um Claras Lippen schwebenden feinen Lächeln, wenn wir uns unterfangen, ihr etwas vorzuquinkelieren, das so tun will als sei es Gesang, unerachtet nur einzelne Töne verworren durcheinander springen.« Es war dem so. Clara hatte die lebenskräftige Fantasie des heitern unbefangenen, kindischen Kindes, ein tiefes weiblich zartes Gemüt, einen gar hellen scharf sichtenden Verstand. Die Nebler und Schwebler hatten bei ihr böses Spiel; denn ohne zu viel zu reden, was überhaupt in Claras schweigsamer Natur nicht lag, sagte ihnen der helle Blick, und jenes feine ironische Lächeln: Lieben Freunde! wie möget ihr mir denn zumuten, daß ich eure verfließende Schattengebilde für wahre Gestalten ansehen soll, mit Leben und Regung? - Clara wurde deshalb von vielen kalt, gefühllos, prosaisch gescholten; aber andere, die das Leben in klarer Tiefe aufgefaßt, liebten ungemein das gemütvolle, verständige, kindliche Mädchen, doch keiner so sehr, als Nathanael, der sich in Wissenschaft und Kunst kräftig und heiter bewegte. Clara hing an dem Geliebten mit ganzer Seele; die ersten Wolkenschatten zogen durch ihr Leben, als er sich von ihr trennte. Mit welchem Entzücken flog sie in seine Arme, als er nun, wie er im letzten Briefe an Lothar es verheißen, wirklich in seiner Vaterstadt ins Zimmer der Mutter eintrat. Es geschah so wie Nathanael geglaubt; denn in dem Augenblick, als er Clara wiedersah, dachte er weder an den Advokaten Coppelius, noch an Claras verständigen Brief, jede Verstimmung war verschwunden.

Nevertheless Nathanael was right when he told his friend Lothair that the repulsive vendor of weather-glasses, Coppola, had exercised a fatal and disturbing influence upon his life. It was quite patent to all; for even during the first few days he showed that he was completely and entirely changed. He gave himself up to gloomy reveries, and moreover acted so strangely; they had never observed anything at all like it in him before. Everything, even his own life, was to him but dreams and presentiments. His constant theme was that every man who delusively imagined himself to be free was merely the plaything of the cruel sport of mysterious powers, and it was vain for man to resist them; he must humbly submit to whatever destiny had decreed for him. He went so far as to maintain that it was foolish to believe that a man could do anything in art or science of his own accord; for the inspiration in which alone any true artistic work could be done did not proceed from the spirit within outwards, but was the result of the operation directed inwards of some Higher Principle existing without and beyond ourselves.

This mystic extravagance was in the highest degree repugnant to Clara's clear intelligent mind, but it seemed vain to enter upon any attempt at refutation. Yet when Nathanael went on to prove that Coppelius was the Evil Principle which had entered into him and taken possession of him at the time he was listening behind the curtain, and that this hateful demon would in some terrible way ruin their happiness, then Clara grew grave and said, "Yes, Nathanael. You are right; Coppelius is an Evil Principle; he can do dreadful things, as bad as could a Satanic power which should assume a living physical form, but only—only if you do not banish him from your mind and thoughts. So long as you believe in him he exists and is at work; your belief in him is his only power." Whereupon Nathanael, quite angry because Clara would only grant the existence of the demon in his own mind, began to dilate at large upon the whole mystic doctrine of devils and awful powers, but Clara abruptly broke off the theme by making, to Nathanael's very great disgust, some quite commonplace remark. Such deep mysteries are sealed books to cold, unsusceptible characters, he thought, without being clearly conscious to himself that he counted Clara amongst these inferior natures, and accordingly he did not remit his efforts to initiate her into these mysteries. In the morning, when she was helping to prepare breakfast, he would take his stand beside her, and read all sorts of mystic books to her, until she begged him—"But, my dear Nathanael, I shall have to scold you as the Evil Principle which exercises a fatal influence upon my coffee. For if I do as you wish, and let things go their own way, and look into your eyes whilst you read, the coffee will all boil over into the fire, and you will none of you get any breakfast." Then Nathanael hastily banged the book to and ran away in great displeasure to his own room.

Recht hatte aber Nathanael doch, als er seinem Freunde Lothar schrieb, daß des widerwärtigen Wetterglashändlers Coppola Gestalt recht feindlich in sein Leben getreten sei. Alle fühlten das, da Nathanael gleich in den ersten Tagen in seinem ganzen Wesen durchaus verändert sich zeigte. Er versank in düstre Träumereien, und trieb es bald so seltsam, wie man es niemals von ihm gewohnt gewesen. Alles, das ganze Leben war ihm Traum und Ahnung geworden; immer sprach er davon, wie jeder Mensch, sich frei wähnend, nur dunklen Mächten zum grausamen Spiel diene, vergeblich lehne man sich dagegen auf, demütig müsse man sich dem fügen, was das Schicksal verhängt habe. Er ging so weit, zu behaupten, daß es töricht sei, wenn man glaube, in Kunst und Wissenschaft nach selbsttätiger Willkür zu schaffen; denn die Begeisterung, in der man nur zu schaffen fähig sei, komme nicht aus dem eignen Innern, sondern sei das Einwirken irgend eines außer uns selbst liegenden höheren Prinzips.

Der verständigen Clara war diese mystische Schwärmerei im höchsten Grade zuwider, doch schien es vergebens, sich auf Widerlegung einzulassen. Nur dann, wenn Nathanael bewies, daß Coppelius das böse Prinzip sei, was ihn in dem Augenblick erfaßt habe, als er hinter dem Vorhange lauschte, und daß dieser widerwärtige Dämon auf entsetzliche Weise ihr Liebesglück stören werde, da wurde Clara sehr ernst und sprach: »Ja Nathanael! du hast recht, Coppelius ist ein böses feindliches Prinzip, er kann Entsetzliches wirken, wie eine teuflische Macht, die sichtbarlich in das Leben trat, aber nur dann, wenn du ihn nicht aus Sinn und Gedanken verbannst. Solange du an ihn glaubst, ist er auch und wirkt, nur dein Glaube ist seine Macht.« - Nathanael, ganz erzürnt, daß Clara die Existenz des Dämons nur in seinem eignen Innern statuiere, wollte dann hervorrücken mit der ganzen mystischen Lehre von Teufeln und grausen Mächten, Clara brach aber verdrüßlich ab, indem sie irgend etwas Gleichgültiges dazwischen schob, zu Nathanaels nicht geringem Ärger. Der dachte, kalten unempfänglichen Gemütern verschließen sich solche tiefe Geheimnisse, ohne sich deutlich bewußt zu sein, daß er Clara eben zu solchen untergeordneten Naturen zähle, weshalb er nicht abließ mit Versuchen, sie in jene Geheimnisse einzuweihen. Am frühen Morgen, wenn Clara das Frühstück bereiten half, stand er bei ihr und las ihr aus allerlei mystischen Büchern vor, daß Clara bat: »Aber lieber Nathanael, wenn ich dich nun das böse Prinzip schelten wollte, das feindlich auf meinen Kaffee wirkt? - Denn, wenn ich, wie du es willst, alles stehen und liegen lassen und dir, indem du liesest, in die Augen schauen soll, so läuft mir der Kaffee ins Feuer und ihr bekommt alle kein Frühstück!« - Nathanael klappte das Buch heftig zu und rannte voll Unmut fort in sein Zimmer.

Formerly he had possessed a peculiar talent for writing pleasing, sparkling tales, which Clara took the greatest delight in listening to; but now his productions were gloomy, unintelligible, and wanting in form, so that, although Clara out of forbearance towards him did not say so, he nevertheless felt how very little interest she took in them. There was nothing that Clara disliked so much as what was tedious; at such times her intellectual sleepiness was not to be overcome; it was betrayed both in her glances and in her words. Nathanael's effusions were, in truth, exceedingly tedious. His ill-humour at Clara's cold prosaic temperament continued to increase; Clara could not conceal her distaste of his dark, gloomy, wearying mysticism; and thus both began to be more and more estranged from each other without exactly being aware of it themselves. The image of the ugly Coppelius had, as Nathanael was obliged to confess to himself, faded considerably in his fancy, and it often cost him great pains to present him in vivid colours in his literary efforts, in which he played the part of the ghoul of Destiny. At length it entered into his head to make his dismal presentiment that Coppelius would ruin his happiness the subject of a poem. He made himself and Clara, united by true love, the central figures, but represented a black hand as being from time to time thrust into their life and plucking out a joy that had blossomed for them. At length, as they were standing at the altar, the terrible Coppelius appeared and touched Clara's lovely eyes, which leapt into Nathanael's own bosom, burning and hissing like bloody sparks. Then Coppelius laid hold upon him, and hurled him into a blazing circle of fire, which spun round with the speed of a whirlwind, and, storming and blustering, dashed away with him. The fearful noise it made was like a furious hurricane lashing the foaming sea-waves until they rise up like black, white-headed giants in the midst of the raging struggle. But through the midst of the savage fury of the tempest he heard Clara's voice calling, "Can you not see me, dear? Coppelius has deceived you; they were not my eyes which burned so in your bosom; they were fiery drops of your own heart's blood. Look at me, I have got my own eyes still." Nathanael thought, "Yes, that is Clara, and I am hers for ever." Then this thought laid a powerful grasp upon the fiery circle so that it stood still, and the riotous turmoil died away rumbling down a dark abyss. Nathanael looked into Clara's eyes; but it was death whose gaze rested so kindly upon him.

Sonst hatte er eine besondere Stärke in anmutigen, lebendigen Erzählungen, die er aufschrieb, und die Clara mit dem innigsten Vergnügen anhörte, jetzt waren seine Dichtungen düster, unverständlich, gestaltlos, so daß, wenn Clara schonend es auch nicht sagte, er doch wohl fühlte, wie wenig sie davon angesprochen wurde. Nichts war für Clara tötender, als das Langweilige; in Blick und Rede sprach sich dann ihre nicht zu besiegende geistige Schläfrigkeit aus. Nathanaels Dichtungen waren in der Tat sehr langweilig. Sein Verdruß über Claras kaltes prosaisches Gemüt stieg höher, Clara konnte ihren Unmut über Nathanaels dunkle, düstere, langweilige Mystik nicht überwinden, und so entfernten beide im Innern sich immer mehr voneinander, ohne es selbst zu bemerken. Die Gestalt des häßlichen Coppelius war, wie Nathanael selbst es sich gestehen mußte, in seiner Fantasie erbleicht und es kostete ihm oft Mühe, ihn in seinen Dichtungen, wo er als grauser Schicksalspopanz auftrat, recht lebendig zu kolorieren. Es kam ihm endlich ein, jene düstre Ahnung, daß Coppelius sein Liebesglück stören werde, zum Gegenstande eines Gedichts zu machen. Er stellte sich und Clara dar, in treuer Liebe verbunden, aber dann und wann war es, als griffe eine schwarze Faust in ihr Leben und risse irgend eine Freude heraus, die ihnen aufgegangen. Endlich, als sie schon am Traualtar stehen, erscheint der entsetzliche Coppelius und berührt Claras holde Augen; die springen in Nathanaels Brust wie blutige Funken sengend und brennend, Coppelius faßt ihn und wirft ihn in einen flammenden Feuerkreis, der sich dreht mit der Schnelligkeit des Sturmes und ihn sausend und brausend fortreißt. Es ist ein Tosen, als wenn der Orkan grimmig hineinpeitscht in die schäumenden Meereswellen, die sich wie schwarze, weißhauptige Riesen emporbäumen in wütendem Kampfe. Aber durch dies wilde Tosen hört er Claras Stimme: »Kannst du mich denn nicht erschauen? Coppelius hat dich getäuscht, das waren ja nicht meine Augen, die so in deiner Brust brannten, das waren ja glühende Tropfen deines eignen Herzbluts - ich habe ja meine Augen, sieh mich doch nur an!« - Nathanael denkt: Das ist Clara, und ich bin ihr eigen ewiglich. - Da ist es, als faßt der Gedanke gewaltig in den Feuerkreis hinein, daß er stehen bleibt, und im schwarzen Abgrund verrauscht dumpf das Getöse. Nathanael blickt in Claras Augen; aber es ist der Tod, der mit Claras Augen ihn freundlich anschaut.

Whilst Nathanael was writing this work he was very quiet and sober-minded; he filed and polished every line, and as he had chosen to submit himself to the limitations of metre, he did not rest until all was pure and musical. When, however, he had at length finished it and read it aloud to himself he was seized with horror and awful dread, and he screamed, "Whose hideous voice is this?" But he soon came to see in it again nothing beyond a very successful poem, and he confidently believed it would enkindle Clara's cold temperament, though to what end she should be thus aroused was not quite clear to his own mind, nor yet what would be the real purpose served by tormenting her with these dreadful pictures, which prophesied a terrible and ruinous end to her affection.

Nathanael and Clara sat in his mother's little garden. Clara was bright and cheerful, since for three entire days her lover, who had been busy writing his poem, had not teased her with his dreams or forebodings. Nathanael, too, spoke in a gay and vivacious way of things of merry import, as he formerly used to do, so that Clara said, "Ah! now I have you again. We have driven away that ugly Coppelius, you see." Then it suddenly occurred to him that he had got the poem in his pocket which he wished to read to her. He at once took out the manuscript and began to read. Clara, anticipating something tedious as usual, prepared to submit to the infliction, and calmly resumed her knitting. But as the sombre clouds rose up darker and darker she let her knitting fall on her lap and sat with her eyes fixed in a set stare upon Nathanael's face. He was quite carried away by his own work, the fire of enthusiasm coloured his cheeks a deep red, and tears started from his eyes. At length he concluded, groaning and showing great lassitude; grasping Clara's hand, he sighed as if he were being utterly melted in inconsolable grief, "Oh! Clara! Clara!" She drew him softly to her heart and said in a low but very grave and impressive tone, "Nathanael, my darling Nathanael, throw that foolish, senseless, stupid thing into the fire." Then Nathanael leapt indignantly to his feet, crying, as he pushed Clara from him, "You damned lifeless automaton!" and rushed away. Clara was cut to the heart, and wept bitterly. "Oh! he has never loved me, for he does not understand me," she sobbed.

Während Nathanael dies dichtete, war er sehr ruhig und besonnen, er feilte und besserte an jeder Zeile und da er sich dem metrischen Zwange unterworfen, ruhte er nicht, bis alles rein und wohlklingend sich fügte. Als er jedoch nun endlich fertig worden, und das Gedicht für sich laut las, da faßte ihn Grausen und wildes Entsetzen und er schrie auf. »Wessen grauenvolle Stimme ist das?« - Bald schien ihm jedoch das Ganze wieder nur eine sehr gelungene Dichtung, und es war ihm, als müsse Claras kaltes Gemüt dadurch entzündet werden, wiewohl er nicht deutlich dachte, wozu denn Clara entzündet, und wozu es denn nun eigentlich führen solle, sie mit den grauenvollen Bildern zu ängstigen, die ein entsetzliches, ihre Liebe zerstörendes Geschick weissagten. Sie, Nathanael und Clara, saßen in der Mutter kleinem Garten, Clara war sehr heiter, weil Nathanael sie seit drei Tagen, in denen er an jener Dichtung schrieb, nicht mit seinen Träumen und Ahnungen geplagt hatte. Auch Nathanael sprach lebhaft und froh von lustigen Dingen wie sonst, so, daß Clara sagte: »Nun erst habe ich dich ganz wieder, siehst du es wohl, wie wir den häßlichen Coppelius vertrieben haben?« Da fiel dem Nathanael erst ein, daß er ja die Dichtung in der Tasche trage, die er habe vorlesen wollen. Er zog auch sogleich die Blätter hervor und fing an zu lesen: Clara, etwas Langweiliges wie gewöhnlich vermutend und sich darein ergebend, fing an, ruhig zu stricken. Aber so wie immer schwärzer und schwärzer das düstre Gewölk aufstieg, ließ sie den Strickstrumpf sinken und blickte starr dem Nathanael ins Auge. Den riß seine Dichtung unaufhaltsam fort, hochrot färbte seine Wangen die innere Glut, Tränen quollen ihm aus den Augen. - Endlich hatte er geschlossen, er stöhnte in tiefer Ermattung - er faßte Claras Hand und seufzte wie aufgelöst in trostlosem Jammer: »Ach! - Clara - Clara!« - Clara drückte ihn sanft an ihren Busen und sagte leise, aber sehr langsam und ernst: »Nathanael - mein herzlieber Nathanael! - wirf das tolle - unsinnige - wahnsinnige Märchen ins Feuer.« Da sprang Nathanael entrüstet auf und rief, Clara von sich stoßend: »Du lebloses, verdammtes Automat!« Er rannte fort, bittre Tränen vergoß die tief verletzte Clara: »Ach er hat mich niemals geliebt, denn er versteht mich nicht«, schluchzte sie laut.

Lothair entered the arbour. Clara was obliged to tell him all that had taken place. He was passionately fond of his sister; and every word of her complaint fell like a spark upon his heart, so that the displeasure which he had long entertained against his dreamy friend Nathanael was kindled into furious anger. He hastened to find Nathanael, and upbraided him in harsh words for his irrational behaviour towards his beloved sister. The fiery Nathanael answered him in the same style. "A fantastic, crack-brained fool," was retaliated with, "A miserable, common, everyday sort of fellow." A meeting was the inevitable consequence. They agreed to meet on the following morning behind the garden-wall, and fight, according to the custom of the students of the place, with sharp rapiers. They went about silent and gloomy; Clara had both heard and seen the violent quarrel, and also observed the fencing-master bring the rapiers in the dusk of the evening. She had a presentiment of what was to happen. They both appeared at the appointed place wrapped up in the same gloomy silence, and threw off their coats. Their eyes flaming with the blood-thirsty light of pugnacity, they were about to begin their contest when Clara burst through the garden door. Sobbing, she screamed, "You savage, terrible men! Cut me down before you attack each other; for how can I live when my lover has slain my brother, or my brother slain my lover?" Lothair let his weapon fall and gazed silently upon the ground, whilst Nathanael's heart was rent with sorrow, and all the affection which he had felt for his lovely Clara in the happiest days of her golden youth was awakened within him. His murderous weapon, too, fell from his hand; he threw himself at Clara's feet. "Oh! can you ever forgive me, my only, my dearly loved Clara? Can you, my dear brother Lothair, also forgive me?" Lothair was touched by his friend's great distress; the three young people embraced each other amidst endless tears, and swore never again to break their bond of love and fidelity.

Nathanael felt as if a heavy burden that had been weighing him down to the earth was now rolled from off him, nay, as if by offering resistance to the dark power which had possessed him, he had rescued his own self from the ruin which had threatened him. Three happy days he now spent amidst the loved ones, and then returned to G——, where he had still a year to stay before settling down in his native town for life.

Everything having reference to Coppelius had been concealed from the mother, for they knew she could not think of him without horror, since she as well as Nathanael believed him to be guilty of causing her husband's death.

Lothar trat in die Laube; Clara mußte ihm erzählen was vorgefallen; er liebte seine Schwester mit ganzer Seele, jedes Wort ihrer Anklage fiel wie ein Funke in sein Inneres, so, daß der Unmut, den er wider den träumerischen Nathanael lange im Herzen getragen, sich entzündete zum wilden Zorn. Er lief zu Nathanael, er warf ihm das unsinnige Betragen gegen die geliebte Schwester in harten Worten vor, die der aufbrausende Nathanael ebenso erwiderte. Ein fantastischer, wahnsinniger Geck wurde mit einem miserablen, gemeinen Alltagsmenschen erwidert. Der Zweikampf war unvermeidlich. Sie beschlossen, sich am folgenden Morgen hinter dem Garten nach dortiger akademischer Sitte mit scharfgeschliffenen Stoßrapieren zu schlagen. Stumm und finster schlichen sie umher, Clara hatte den heftigen Streit gehört und gesehen, daß der Fechtmeister in der Dämmerung die Rapiere brachte. Sie ahnte was geschehen sollte. Auf dem Kampfplatz angekommen hatten Lothar und Nathanael soeben düster-schweigend die Röcke abgeworfen, blutdürstige Kampflust im brennenden Auge wollten sie gegeneinander ausfallen, als Clara durch die Gartentür herbeistürzte. Schluchzend rief sie laut: »Ihr wilden entsetzlichen Menschen! - stoßt mich nur gleich nieder, ehe ihr euch anfallt; denn wie soll ich denn länger leben auf der Welt, wenn der Geliebte den Bruder, oder wenn der Bruder den Geliebten ermordet hat!« - Lothar ließ die Waffe sinken und sah schweigend zur Erde nieder, aber in Nathanaels Innern ging in herzzerreißender Wehmut alle Liebe wieder auf, wie er sie jemals in der herrlichen Jugendzeit schönsten Tagen für die holde Clara empfunden. Das Mordgewehr entfiel seiner Hand, er stürzte zu Claras Füßen. »Kannst du mir denn jemals verzeihen, du meine einzige, meine herzgeliebte Clara! - Kannst du mir verzeihen, mein herzlieber Bruder Lothar!« - Lothar wurde gerührt von des Freundes tiefem Schmerz; unter tausend Tränen umarmten sich die drei versöhnten Menschen und schwuren, nicht voneinander zu lassen in steter Liebe und Treue.

Dem Nathanael war es zumute, als sei eine schwere Last, die ihn zu Boden gedrückt, von ihm abgewälzt, ja als habe er, Widerstand leistend der finstern Macht, die ihn befangen, sein ganzes Sein, dem Vernichtung drohte, gerettet. Noch drei selige Tage verlebte er bei den Lieben, dann kehrte er zurück nach G., wo er noch ein Jahr zu bleiben, dann aber auf immer nach seiner Vaterstadt zurückzukehren gedachte.

Der Mutter war alles, was sich auf Coppelius bezog, verschwiegen worden; denn man wußte, daß sie nicht ohne Entsetzen an ihn denken konnte, weil sie, wie Nathanael, ihm den Tod ihres Mannes schuld gab.

When Nathanael came to the house where he lived he was greatly astonished to find it burnt down to the ground, so that nothing but the bare outer walls were left standing amidst a heap of ruins. Although the fire had broken out in the laboratory of the chemist who lived on the ground-floor, and had therefore spread upwards, some of Nathanael's bold, active friends had succeeded in time in forcing a way into his room in the upper storey and saving his books and manuscripts and instruments. They had carried them all uninjured into another house, where they engaged a room for him; this he now at once took possession of. That he lived opposite Professor Spalanzani did not strike him particularly, nor did it occur to him as anything more singular that he could, as he observed, by looking out of his window, see straight into the room where Olimpia often sat alone. Her figure he could plainly distinguish, although her features were uncertain and confused. It did at length occur to him, however, that she remained for hours together in the same position in which he had first discovered her through the glass door, sitting at a little table without any occupation whatever, and it was evident that she was constantly gazing across in his direction. He could not but confess to himself that he had never seen a finer figure. However, with Clara mistress of his heart, he remained perfectly unaffected by Olimpia's stiffness and apathy; and it was only occasionally that he sent a fugitive glance over his compendium across to her—that was all.

He was writing to Clara; a light tap came at the door. At his summons to "Come in," Coppola's repulsive face appeared peeping in. Nathanael felt his heart beat with trepidation; but, recollecting what Spalanzani had told him about his fellow-countryman Coppola, and what he had himself so faithfully promised his beloved in respect to the Sandman Coppelius, he was ashamed at himself for this childish fear of spectres. Accordingly, he controlled himself with an effort, and said, as quietly and as calmly as he possibly could, "I don't want to buy any weather-glasses, my good friend; you had better go elsewhere." Then Coppola came right into the room, and said in a hoarse voice, screwing up his wide mouth into a hideous smile, whilst his little eyes flashed keenly from beneath his long grey eyelashes, "What! Nee weather-gless? Nee weather-gless? 've got foine oyes as well—foine oyes!" Affrighted, Nathanael cried, "You stupid man, how can you have eyes?—eyes—eyes?" But Coppola, laying aside his weather-glasses, thrust his hands into his big coat-pockets and brought out several spy-glasses and spectacles, and put them on the table. "Theer! Theer! Spect'cles! Spect'cles to put 'n nose! Them's my oyes—foine oyes." And he continued to produce more and more spectacles from his pockets until the table began to gleam and flash all over. Thousands of eyes were looking and blinking convulsively, and staring up at Nathanael; he could not avert his gaze from the table. Coppola went on heaping up his spectacles, whilst wilder and ever wilder burning flashes crossed through and through each other and darted their blood-red rays into Nathanael's breast.

Wie erstaunte Nathanael, als er in seine Wohnung wollte und sah, daß das ganze Haus niedergebrannt war, so daß aus dem Schutthaufen nur die nackten Feuermauern hervorragten. Unerachtet das Feuer in dem Laboratorium des Apothekers, der im untern Stocke wohnte, ausgebrochen war, das Haus daher von unten herauf gebrannt hatte, so war es doch den kühnen, rüstigen Freunden gelungen, noch zu rechter Zeit in Nathanaels im obern Stock gelegenes Zimmer zu dringen, und Bücher, Manuskripte, Instrumente zu retten. Alles hatten sie unversehrt in ein anderes Haus getragen, und dort ein Zimmer in Beschlag genommen, welches Nathanael nun sogleich bezog. Nicht sonderlich achtete er darauf, daß er dem Professor Spalanzani gegenüber wohnte, und ebensowenig schien es ihm etwas Besonderes, als er bemerkte, daß er aus seinem Fenster gerade hinein in das Zimmer blickte, wo oft Olimpia einsam saß, so, daß er ihre Figur deutlich erkennen konnte, wiewohl die Züge des Gesichts undeutlich und verworren blieben. Wohl fiel es ihm endlich auf, daß Olimpia oft stundenlang in derselben Stellung, wie er sie einst durch die Glastüre entdeckte, ohne irgend eine Beschäftigung an einem kleinen Tische saß und daß sie offenbar unverwandten Blickes nach ihm herüberschaute; er mußte sich auch selbst gestehen, daß er nie einen schöneren Wuchs gesehen; indessen, Clara im Herzen, blieb ihm die steife, starre Olimpia höchst gleichgültig und nur zuweilen sah er flüchtig über sein Kompendium herüber nach der schönen Bildsäule, das war alles. - Eben schrieb er an Clara, als es leise an die Türe klopfte; sie öffnete sich auf seinen Zuruf und Coppolas widerwärtiges Gesicht sah hinein. Nathanael fühlte sich im Innersten erbeben; eingedenk dessen, was ihm Spalanzani über den Landsmann Coppola gesagt und was er auch rücksichts des Sandmanns Coppelius der Geliebten so heilig versprochen, schämte er sich aber selbst seiner kindischen Gespensterfurcht, nahm sich mit aller Gewalt zusammen und sprach so sanft und gelassen, als möglich: »Ich kaufe kein Wetterglas, mein lieber Freund! gehen Sie nur!« Da trat aber Coppola vollends in die Stube und sprach mit heiserem Ton, indem sich das weite Maul zum häßlichen Lachen verzog und die kleinen Augen unter den grauen langen Wimpern stechend hervorfunkelten: »Ei, nix Wetterglas, nix Wetterglas! - hab auch sköne Oke - sköne Oke!« - Entsetzt rief Nathanael: »Toller Mensch, wie kannst du Augen haben? - Augen - Augen? -« Aber in dem Augenblick hatte Coppola seine Wettergläser beiseite gesetzt, griff in die weiten Rocktaschen und holte Lorgnetten und Brillen heraus, die er auf den Tisch legte. - »Nu - Nu - Brill - Brill auf der Nas su setze, das sein meine Oke - sköne Oke!« - Und damit holte er immer mehr und mehr Brillen heraus, so, daß es auf dem ganzen Tisch seltsam zu flimmern und zu funkeln begann. Tausend Augen blickten und zuckten krampfhaft und starrten auf zum Nathanael; aber er konnte nicht wegschauen von dem Tisch, und immer mehr Brillen legte Coppola hin, und immer wilder und wilder sprangen flammende Blicke durcheinander und schossen ihre blutrote Strahlen in Nathanaels Brust.

Quite overcome, and frantic with terror, he shouted, "Stop! stop! you terrible man!" and he seized Coppola by the arm, which he had again thrust into his pocket in order to bring out still more spectacles, although the whole table was covered all over with them. With a harsh disagreeable laugh Coppola gently freed himself; and with the words "So! went none! Well, here foine gless!" he swept all his spectacles together, and put them back into his coat-pockets, whilst from a breast-pocket he produced a great number of larger and smaller perspectives. As soon as the spectacles were gone Nathanael recovered his equanimity again; and, bending his thoughts upon Clara, he clearly discerned that the gruesome incubus had proceeded only from himself, as also that Coppola was a right honest mechanician and optician, and far from being Coppelius's dreaded double and ghost And then, besides, none of the glasses which Coppola now placed on the table had anything at all singular about them, at least nothing so weird as the spectacles; so, in order to square accounts with himself, Nathanael now really determined to buy something of the man. He took up a small, very beautifully cut pocket perspective, and by way of proving it looked through the window. Never before in his life had he had a glass in his hands that brought out things so clearly and sharply and distinctly. Involuntarily he directed the glass upon Spalanzani's room; Olimpia sat at the little table as usual, her arms laid upon it and her hands folded. Now he saw for the first time the regular and exquisite beauty of her features. The eyes, however, seemed to him to have a singular look of fixity and lifelessness. But as he continued to look closer and more carefully through the glass he fancied a light like humid moonbeams came into them. It seemed as if their power of vision was now being enkindled; their glances shone with ever-increasing vivacity. Nathanael remained standing at the window as if glued to the spot by a wizard's spell, his gaze rivetted unchangeably upon the divinely beautiful Olimpia. A coughing and shuffling of the feet awakened him out of his enchaining dream, as it were. Coppola stood behind him, "Tre zechini" (three ducats). Nathanael had completely forgotten the optician; he hastily paid the sum demanded. "Ain't 't? Foine gless? foine gless?" asked Coppola in his harsh unpleasant voice, smiling sardonically. "Yes, yes, yes," rejoined Nathanael impatiently; "adieu, my good friend." But Coppola did not leave the room without casting many peculiar side-glances upon Nathanael; and the young student heard him laughing loudly on the stairs. "Ah well!" thought he, "he's laughing at me because I've paid him too much for this little perspective—because I've given him too much money—that's it" As he softly murmured these words he fancied he detected a gasping sigh as of a dying man stealing awfully through the room; his heart stopped beating with fear. But to be sure he had heaved a deep sigh himself; it was quite plain. "Clara is quite right," said he to himself, "in holding me to be an incurable ghost-seer; and yet it's very ridiculous—ay, more than ridiculous, that the stupid thought of having paid Coppola too much for his glass should cause me this strange anxiety; I can't see any reason for it."

Übermannt von tollem Entsetzen schrie er auf.- »Halt ein! halt ein, fürchterlicher Mensch!« - Er hatte Coppola, der eben in die Tasche griff, um noch mehr Brillen herauszubringen, unerachtet schon der ganze Tisch überdeckt war, beim Arm festgepackt. Coppola machte sich mit heiserem widrigen Lachen sanft los und mit den Worten: »Ah! - nix für Sie - aber hier sköne Glas« - hatte er alle Brillen zusammengerafft, eingesteckt und aus der Seitentasche des Rocks eine Menge großer und kleiner Perspektive hervorgeholt. Sowie die Brillen fort waren, wurde Nathanael ganz ruhig und an Clara denkend sah er wohl ein, daß der entsetzliche Spuk nur aus seinem Innern hervorgegangen, sowie daß Coppola ein höchst ehrlicher Mechanikus und Optikus, keineswegs aber Coppelii verfluchter Doppeltgänger und Revenant sein könne. Zudem hatten alle Gläser, die Coppola nun auf den Tisch gelegt, gar nichts Besonderes, am wenigsten so etwas Gespenstisches wie die Brillen und, um alles wieder gutzumachen, beschloß Nathanael dem Coppola jetzt wirklich etwas abzukaufen. Er ergriff ein kleines sehr sauber gearbeitetes Taschenperspektiv und sah, um es zu prüfen, durch das Fenster. Noch im Leben war ihm kein Glas vorgekommen, das die Gegenstände so rein, scharf und deutlich dicht vor die Augen rückte. Unwillkürlich sah er hinein in Spalanzanis Zimmer; Olimpia saß, wie gewöhnlich, vor dem kleinen Tisch, die Arme darauf gelegt, die Hände gefaltet. - Nun erschaute Nathanael erst Olimpias wunderschön geformtes Gesicht. Nur die Augen schienen ihm gar seltsam starr und tot. Doch wie er immer schärfer und schärfer durch das Glas hinschaute, war es, als gingen in Olimpias Augen feuchte Mondesstrahlen auf. Es schien, als wenn nun erst die Sehkraft entzündet würde; immer lebendiger und lebendiger flammten die Blicke. Nathanael lag wie festgezaubert im Fenster, immer fort und fort die himmlischschöne Olimpia betrachtend. Ein Räuspern und Scharren weckte ihn, wie aus tiefem Traum. Coppola stand hinter ihm: »Tre Zechini - drei Dukat« - Nathanael hatte den Optikus rein vergessen, rasch zahlte er das Verlangte. »Nick so? - sköne Glas - sköne Glas!« frug Coppola mit seiner widerwärtigen heisern Stimme und dem hämischen Lächeln. »Ja ja, ja!« erwiderte Nathanael verdrießlich. »Adieu, lieber Freund!« - Coppola verließ nicht ohne viele seltsame Seitenblicke auf Nathanael, das Zimmer. Er hörte ihn auf der Treppe laut lachen. »Nun ja«, meinte Nathanael, »er lacht mich aus, weil ich ihm das kleine Perspektiv gewiß viel zu teuer bezahlt habe - zu teuer bezahlt!« - Indem er diese Worte leise sprach, war es, als halle ein tiefer Todesseufzer grauenvoll durch das Zimmer, Nathanaels Atem stockte vor innerer Angst. - Er hatte ja aber selbst so aufgeseufzt, das merkte er wohl. »Clara«, sprach er zu sich selber, »hat wohl recht, daß sie mich für einen abgeschmackten Geisterseher hält; aber närrisch ist es doch - ach wohl mehr, als närrisch, daß mich der dumme Gedanke, ich hätte das Glas dem Coppola zu teuer bezahlt, noch jetzt so sonderbar ängstigt; den Grund davon sehe ich gar nicht ein.«

Now he sat down to finish his letter to Clara; but a glance through the window showed him Olimpia still in her former posture. Urged by an irresistible impulse he jumped up and seized Coppola's perspective; nor could he tear himself away from the fascinating Olimpia until his friend and brother Siegmund called for him to go to Professor Spalanzani's lecture. The curtains before the door of the all-important room were closely drawn, so that he could not see Olimpia. Nor could he even see her from his own room during the two following days, notwithstanding that he scarcely ever left his window, and maintained a scarce interrupted watch through Coppola's perspective upon her room. On the third day curtains even were drawn across the window. Plunged into the depths of despair,—goaded by longing and ardent desire, he hurried outside the walls of the town. Olimpia's image hovered about his path in the air and stepped forth out of the bushes, and peeped up at him with large and lustrous eyes from the bright surface of the brook. Clara's image was completely faded from his mind; he had no thoughts except for Olimpia. He uttered his love-plaints aloud and in a lachrymose tone, "Oh! my glorious, noble star of love, have you only risen to vanish again, and leave me in the darkness and hopelessness of night?"

Returning home, he became aware that there was a good deal of noisy bustle going on in Spalanzani's house. All the doors stood wide open; men were taking in all kinds of gear and furniture; the windows of the first floor were all lifted off their hinges; busy maid-servants with immense hair-brooms were driving backwards and forwards dusting and sweeping, whilst within could be heard the knocking and hammering of carpenters and upholsterers. Utterly astonished, Nathanael stood still in the street; then Siegmund joined him, laughing, and said, "Well, what do you say to our old Spalanzani?" Nathanael assured him that he could not say anything, since he knew not what it all meant; to his great astonishment, he could hear, however, that they were turning the quiet gloomy house almost inside out with their dusting and cleaning and making of alterations. Then he learned from Siegmund that Spalanzani intended giving a great concert and ball on the following day, and that half the university was invited. It was generally reported that Spalanzani was going to let his daughter Olimpia, whom he had so long so jealously guarded from every eye, make her first appearance.

Jetzt setzte er sich hin, um den Brief an Clara zu enden, aber ein Blick durchs Fenster überzeugte ihn, daß Olimpia noch dasäße und im Augenblick, wie von unwiderstehlicher Gewalt getrieben, sprang er auf, ergriff Coppolas Perspektiv und konnte nicht los von Olimpias verführerischem Anblick, bis ihn Freund und Bruder Siegmund abrief ins Kollegium bei dem Professor Spalanzani. Die Gardine vor dem verhängnisvollen Zimmer war dicht zugezogen, er konnte Olimpia ebensowenig hier, als die beiden folgenden Tage hindurch in ihrem Zimmer, entdecken, unerachtet er kaum das Fenster verließ und fortwährend durch Coppolas Perspektiv hinüberschaute. Am dritten Tage wurden sogar die Fenster verhängt. Ganz verzweifelt und getrieben von Sehnsucht und glühendem Verlangen lief er hinaus vors Tor. Olimpias Gestalt schwebte vor ihm her in den Lüften und trat aus dem Gebüsch, und guckte ihn an mit großen strahlenden Augen, aus dem hellen Bach. Claras Bild war ganz aus seinem Innern gewichen, er dachte nichts, als Olimpia und klagte ganz laut und weinerlich: »Ach du mein hoher herrlicher Liebesstern, bist du mir denn nur aufgegangen, um gleich wieder zu verschwinden, und mich zu lassen in finstrer hoffnungsloser Nacht?«

Als er zurückkehren wollte in seine Wohnung, wurde er in Spalanzanis Hause ein geräuschvolles Treiben gewahr. Die Türen standen offen, man trug allerlei Geräte hinein, die Fenster des ersten Stocks waren ausgehoben, geschäftige Mägde kehrten und stäubten mit großen Haarbesen hin- und herfahrend, inwendig klopften und hämmerten Tischler und Tapezierer. Nathanael blieb in vollem Erstaunen auf der Straße stehen; da trat Siegmund lachend zu ihm und sprach: »Nun, was sagst du zu unserem alten Spalanzani?« Nathanael versicherte, daß er gar nichts sagen könne, da er durchaus nichts vom Professor wisse, vielmehr mit großer Verwunderung wahrnehme, wie in dem stillen düstern Hause ein tolles Treiben und Wirtschaften losgegangen; da erfuhr er denn von Siegmund, daß Spalanzani morgen ein großes Fest geben wolle, Konzert und Ball, und daß die halbe Universität eingeladen sei. Allgemein verbreite man, daß Spalanzani seine Tochter Olimpia, die er so lange jedem menschlichen Auge recht ängstlich entzogen, zum erstenmal erscheinen lassen werde.

Nathanael received an invitation. At the appointed hour, when the carriages were rolling up and the lights were gleaming brightly in the decorated halls, he went across to the Professor's, his heart beating high with expectation. The company was both numerous and brilliant. Olimpia was richly and tastefully dressed. One could not but admire her figure and the regular beauty of her features. The striking inward curve of her back, as well as the wasp-like small-ness of her waist, appeared to be the result of too-tight lacing. There was something stiff and measured in her gait and bearing that made an unfavourable impression upon many; it was ascribed to the constraint imposed upon her by the company. The concert began. Olimpia played on the piano with great skill; and sang as skilfully an aria di bravura, in a voice which was, if anything, almost too sharp, but clear as glass bells. Nathanael was transported with delight; he stood in the background farthest from her, and owing to the blinding lights could not quite distinguish her features. So, without being observed, he took Coppola's glass out of his pocket, and directed it upon the beautiful Olimpia. Oh! then he perceived how her yearning eyes sought him, how every note only reached its full purity in the loving glance which penetrated to and inflamed his heart. Her artificial roulades seemed to him to be the exultant cry towards heaven of the soul refined by love; and when at last, after the cadenza, the long trill rang shrilly and loudly through the hall, he felt as if he were suddenly grasped by burning arms and could no longer control himself,—he could not help shouting aloud in his mingled pain and delight, "Olimpia!" All eyes were turned upon him; many people laughed. The face of the cathedral organist wore a still more gloomy look than it had done before, but all he said was, "Very well!"

The concert came to an end, and the ball began. Oh! to dance with her—with her—that was now the aim of all Nathanael's wishes, of all his desires. But how should he have courage to request her, the queen of the ball, to grant him the honour of a dance? And yet he couldn't tell how it came about, just as the dance began, he found himself standing close beside her, nobody having as yet asked her to be his partner; so, with some difficulty stammering out a few words, he grasped her hand. It was cold as ice; he shook with an awful, frosty shiver. But, fixing his eyes upon her face, he saw that her glance was beaming upon him with love and longing, and at the same moment he thought that the pulse began to beat in her cold hand, and the warm life-blood to course through her veins. And passion burned more intensely in his own heart also; he threw his arm round her beautiful waist and whirled her round the hall. He had always thought that he kept good and accurate time in dancing, but from the perfectly rhythmical evenness with which Olimpia danced, and which frequently put him quite out, he perceived how very faulty his own time really was. Notwithstand-ing, he would not dance with any other lady; and everybody else who ap-proached Olimpia to call upon her for a dance, he would have liked to kill on the spot.

Nathanael fand eine Einladungskarte und ging mit hochklopfendem Herzen zur bestimmten Stunde, als schon die Wagen rollten und die Lichter in den geschmückten Sälen schimmerten, zum Professor. Die Gesellschaft war zahlreich und glänzend. Olimpia erschien sehr reich und geschmackvoll gekleidet. Man mußte ihr schöngeformtes Gesicht, ihren Wuchs bewundern. Der etwas seltsam eingebogene Rücken, die wespenartige Dünne des Leibes schien von zu starkem Einschnüren bewirkt zu sein. In Schritt und Stellung hatte sie etwas Abgemessenes und Steifes, das manchem unangenehm auffiel; man schrieb es dem Zwange zu, den ihr die Gesellschaft auflegte. Das Konzert begann. Olimpia spielte den Flügel mit großer Fertigkeit und trug ebenso eine Bravour-Arie mit heller, beinahe schneidender Glasglockenstimme vor. Nathanael war ganz entzückt; er stand in der hintersten Reihe und konnte im blendenden Kerzenlicht Olimpias Züge nicht ganz erkennen. Ganz unvermerkt nahm er deshalb Coppolas Glas hervor und schaute hin nach der schönen Olimpia. Ach! - da wurde er gewahr, wie sie voll Sehnsucht nach ihm herübersah, wie jeder Ton erst deutlich aufging in dem Liebesblick, der zündend sein Inneres durchdrang. Die künstlichen Rouladen schienen dem Nathanael das Himmelsjauchzen des in Liebe verklärten Gemüts, und als nun endlich nach der Kadenz der lange Trillo recht schmetternd durch den Saal gellte, konnte er wie von glühenden Ärmen plötzlich erfaßt sich nicht mehr halten, er mußte vor Schmerz und Entzücken laut aufschreien: »Olimpia!« - Alle sahen sich um nach ihm, manche lachten. Der Domorganist schnitt aber noch ein finstreres Gesicht, als vorher und sagte bloß: »Nun nun!« - Das Konzert war zu Ende, der Ball fing an. »Mit ihr zu tanzen! - mit ihr!« das war nun dem Nathanael das Ziel aller Wünsche, alles Strebens; aber wie sich erheben zu dem Mut, sie, die Königin des Festes, aufzufordern? Doch! - er selbst wußte nicht wie es geschah, daß er, als schon der Tanz angefangen, dicht neben Olimpia stand, die noch nicht aufgefordert worden, und daß er, kaum vermögend einige Worte zu stammeln, ihre Hand ergriff. Eiskalt war Olimpias Hand, er fühlte sich durchbebt von grausigem Todesfrost, er starrte Olimpia ins Auge, das strahlte ihm voll Liebe und Sehnsucht entgegen und in dem Augenblick war es auch, als fingen an in der kalten Hand Pulse zu schlagen und des Lebensblutes Ströme zu glühen. Und auch in Nathanaels Innerm glühte höher auf die Liebeslust, er umschlang die schöne Olimpia und durchflog mit ihr die Reihen. - Er glaubte sonst recht taktmäßig getanzt zu haben, aber an der ganz eignen rhythmischen Festigkeit, womit Olimpia tanzte und die ihn oft ordentlich aus der Haltung brachte, merkte er bald, wie sehr ihm der Takt gemangelt. Er wollte jedoch mit keinem andern Frauenzimmer mehr tanzen und hätte jeden, der sich Olimpia näherte, um sie aufzufordern, nur gleich ermorden mögen.

This, however, only happened twice; to his astonishment Olimpia remained after this without a partner, and he failed not on each occasion to take her out again. If Nathanael had been able to see anything else except the beautiful Olimpia, there would inevitably have been a good deal of unpleasant quarrelling and strife; for it was evident that Olimpia was the object of the smothered laughter only with difficulty suppressed, which was heard in various corners amongst the young people; and they followed her with very curious looks, but nobody knew for what reason. Nathanael, excited by dancing and the plentiful supply of wine he had consumed, had laid aside the shyness which at other times characterised him. He sat beside Olimpia, her hand in his own, and declared his love enthusiastically and passionately in words which neither of them understood, neither he nor Olimpia. And yet she perhaps did, for she sat with her eyes fixed unchangeably upon his, sighing repeatedly, "Ach! Ach! Ach!" Upon this Nathanael would answer, "Oh, you glorious heavenly lady! You ray from the promised paradise of love! Oh! what a profound soul you have! my whole being is mirrored in it!" and a good deal more in the same strain. But Olimpia only continued to sigh "Ach! Ach!" again and again.

Professor Spalanzani passed by the two happy lovers once or twice, and smiled with a look of peculiar satisfaction. All at once it seemed to Nathanael, albeit he was far away in a different world, as if it were growing perceptibly darker down below at Professor Spalanzani's. He looked about him, and to his very great alarm became aware that there were only two lights left burning in the hall, and they were on the point of going out. The music and dancing had long ago ceased. "We must part—part!" he cried, wildly and despairingly; he kissed Olimpia's hand; he bent down to her mouth, but ice-cold lips met his burning ones. As he touched her cold hand, he felt his heart thrilled with awe; the legend of "The Dead Bride" shot suddenly through his mind. But Olimpia had drawn him closer to her, and the kiss appeared to warm her lips into vitality. Professor Spalanzani strode slowly through the empty apartment, his footsteps giving a hollow echo; and his figure had, as the flickering shadows played about him, a ghostly, awful appearance. "Do you love me? Do you love me, Olimpia? Only one little word—Do you love me?" whispered Nathanael, but she only sighed, "Ach! Ach!" as she rose to her feet. "Yes, you are my lovely, glorious star of love," said Nathanael, "and will shine for ever, purifying and ennobling my heart" "Ach! Ach!" replied Olimpia, as she moved along. Nathanael followed her; they stood before the Professor. "You have had an extraordinarily animated conversation with my daughter," said he, smiling; "well, well, my dear Mr. Nathanael, if you find pleasure in talking to the stupid girl, I am sure I shall be glad for you to come and do so." Nathanael took his leave, his heart singing and leaping in a perfect delirium of happiness.

Doch nur zweimal geschah dies, zu seinem Erstaunen blieb darauf Olimpia bei jedem Tanze sitzen und er ermangelte nicht, immer wieder sie aufzuziehen. Hätte Nathanael außer der schönen Olimpia noch etwas andres zu sehen vermocht, so wäre allerlei fataler Zank und Streit unvermeidlich gewesen; denn offenbar ging das halbleise, mühsam unterdrückte Gelächter, was sich in diesem und jenem Winkel unter den jungen Leuten erhob, auf die schöne Olimpia, die sie mit ganz kuriosen Blicken verfolgten, man konnte gar nicht wissen, warum? Durch den Tanz und durch den reichlich genossenen Wein erhitzt, hatte Nathanael alle ihm sonst eigne Scheu abgelegt. Er saß neben Olimpia, ihre Hand in der seinigen und sprach hochentflammt und begeistert von seiner Liebe in Worten, die keiner verstand, weder er, noch Olimpia. Doch diese vielleicht; denn sie sah ihm unverrückt ins Auge und seufzte einmal übers andere: »Ach - Ach - Ach!« - worauf denn Nathanael also sprach: »O du herrliche, himmlische Frau! - du Strahl aus dem verheißenen Jenseits der Liebe - du tiefes Gemüt, in dem sich mein ganzes Sein spiegelt« und noch mehr dergleichen, aber Olimpia seufzte bloß immer wieder: »Ach, Ach!« - Der Professor Spalanzani ging einigemal bei den Glücklichen vorüber und lächelte sie ganz seltsam zufrieden an. Dem Nathanael schien es, unerachtet er sich in einer ganz andern Welt befand, mit einemmal, als würd es hienieden beim Professor Spalanzani merklich finster; er schaute um sich und wurde zu seinem nicht geringen Schreck gewahr, daß eben die zwei letzten Lichter in dem leeren Saal herniederbrennen und ausgehen wollten. Längst hatten Musik und Tanz aufgehört. »Trennung, Trennung«, schrie er ganz wild und verzweifelt, er küßte Olimpias Hand, er neigte sich zu ihrem Munde, eiskalte Lippen begegneten seinen glühenden! - So wie, als er Olimpias kalte Hand berührte, fühlte er sich von innerem Grausen erfaßt, die Legende von der toten Braut ging ihm plötzlich durch den Sinn; aber fest hatte ihn Olimpia an sich gedrückt, und in dem Kuß schienen die Lippen zum Leben zu erwarmen. - Der Professor Spalanzani schritt langsam durch den leeren Saal, seine Schritte klangen hohl wieder und seine Figur, von flackernden Schlagschatten umspielt, hatte ein grauliches gespenstisches Ansehen. »Liebst du mich - liebst du mich Olimpia? - Nur dies Wort! - Liebst du mich?« So flüsterte Nathanael, aber Olimpia seufzte, indem sie aufstand, nur: »Ach - Ach!« - »Ja du mein holder, herrlicher Liebesstern«, sprach Nathanael, »bist mir aufgegangen und wirst leuchten, wirst verklären mein Inneres immerdar!« - »Ach, ach!« replizierte Olimpia fortschreitend. Nathanael folgte ihr, sie standen vor dem Professor. »Sie haben sich außerordentlich lebhaft mit meiner Tochter unterhalten«, sprach dieser lächelnd: »Nun, nun, lieber Herr Nathanael, finden Sie Geschmack daran, mit dem blöden Mädchen zu konvergieren, so sollen mir Ihre Besuche willkommen sein.« - Einen ganzen hellen strahlenden Himmel in der Brust schied Nathanael von dannen.

During the next few days Spalanzani's ball was the general topic of conversation. Although the Professor had done everything to make the thing a splendid success, yet certain gay spirits related more than one thing that had occurred which was quite irregular and out of order. They were especially keen in pulling Olimpia to pieces for her taciturnity and rigid stiffness; in spite of her beautiful form they alleged that she was hopelessly stupid, and in this fact they discerned the reason why Spalanzani had so long kept her concealed from publicity. Nathanael heard all this with inward wrath, but nevertheless he held his tongue; for, thought he, would it indeed be worth while to prove to these fellows that it is their own stupidity which prevents them from appreciating Olimpia's profound and brilliant parts? One day Siegmund said to him, "Pray, brother, have the kindness to tell me how you, a sensible fellow, came to lose your head over that Miss Wax-face—that wooden doll across there?" Nathanael was about to fly into a rage, but he recollected himself and replied, "Tell me, Siegmund, how came it that Olimpia's divine charms could escape your eye, so keenly alive as it always is to beauty, and your acute perception as well? But Heaven be thanked for it, otherwise I should have had you for a rival, and then the blood of one of us would have had to be spilled." Siegmund, perceiving how matters stood with his friend, skilfully interposed and said, after remarking that all argument with one in love about the object of his affections was out of place, "Yet it's very strange that several of us have formed pretty much the same opinion about Olimpia. We think she is—you won't take it ill, brother?— that she is singularly statuesque and soulless. Her figure is regular, and so are her features, that can't be gainsaid; and if her eyes were not so utterly devoid of life, I may say, of the power of vision, she might pass for a beauty. She is strangely measured in her movements, they all seem as if they were dependent upon some wound-up clock-work. Her playing and singing has the disagreeably perfect, but insensitive time of a singing machine, and her dancing is the same. We felt quite afraid of this Olimpia, and did not like to have anything to do with her; she seemed to us to be only acting like a living creature, and as if there was some secret at the bottom of it all." Nathanael did not give way to the bitter feelings which threatened to master him at these words of Siegmund's; he fought down and got the better of his displeasure, and merely said, very earnestly, "You cold prosaic fellows may very well be afraid of her. It is only to its like that the poetically organised spirit unfolds itself. Upon me alone did her loving glances fall, and through my mind and thoughts alone did they radiate; and only in her love can I find my own self again. Perhaps, however, she doesn't do quite right not to jabber a lot of nonsense and stupid talk like other shallow people. It is true, she speaks but few words; but the few words she docs speak are genuine hieroglyphs of the inner world of Love and of the higher cognition of the intellectual life revealed in the intuition of the Eternal beyond the grave. But you have no understanding for all these things, and I am only wasting words."

Spalanzanis Fest war der Gegenstand des Gesprächs in den folgenden Tagen. Unerachtet der Professor alles getan hatte, recht splendid zu erscheinen, so wußten doch die lustigen Köpfe von allerlei Unschicklichem und Sonderbarem zu erzählen, das sich begeben, und vorzüglich fiel man über die todstarre, stumme Olimpia her, der man, ihres schönen Äußern unerachtet, totalen Stumpfsinn andichten und darin die Ursache finden wollte, warum Spalanzani sie so lange verborgen gehalten. Nathanael vernahm das nicht ohne innern Grimm, indessen schwieg er; denn, dachte er, würde es wohl verlohnen, diesen Burschen zu beweisen, daß eben ihr eigner Stumpfsinn es ist, der sie Olimpias tiefes herrliches Gemüt zu erkennen hindert? »Tu mir den Gefallen, Bruder«, sprach eines Tages Siegmund, »tu mir den Gefallen und sage, wie es dir gescheuten Kerl möglich war, dich in das Wachsgesicht, in die Holzpuppe da drüben zu vergaffen?« Nathanael wollte zornig auffahren, doch schnell besann er sich und erwiderte: »Sage du mir Siegmund, wie deinem, sonst alles Schöne klar auffassenden Blick, deinem regen Sinn, Olimpias himmlischer Liebreiz entgehen konnte? Doch eben deshalb habe ich, Dank sei es dem Geschick, dich nicht zum Nebenbuhler; denn sonst müßte einer von uns blutend fallen.« Siegmund merkte wohl, wie es mit dem Freunde stand, lenkte geschickt ein, und fügte, nachdem er geäußert, daß in der Liebe niemals über den Gegenstand zu richten sei, hinzu: »Wunderlich ist es doch, daß viele von uns über Olimpia ziemlich gleich urteilen. Sie ist uns - nimm es nicht übel, Bruder! - auf seltsame Weise starr und seelenlos erschienen. Ihr Wuchs ist regelmäßig, so wie ihr Gesicht, das ist wahr! - Sie könnte für schön gelten, wenn ihr Blick nicht so ganz ohne Lebensstrahl, ich möchte sagen, ohne Sehkraft wäre. Ihr Schritt ist sonderbar abgemessen, jede Bewegung scheint durch den Gang eines aufgezogenen Räderwerks bedingt. Ihr Spiel, ihr Singen hat den unangenehm richtigen geistlosen Takt der singenden Maschine und ebenso ist ihr Tanz. Uns ist diese Olimpia ganz unheimlich geworden, wir mochten nichts mit ihr zu schaffen haben, es war uns als tue sie nur so wie ein lebendiges Wesen und doch habe es mit ihr eine eigne Bewandtnis.« - Nathanael gab sich dem bittern Gefühl, das ihn bei diesen Worten Siegmunds ergreifen wollte, durchaus nicht hin, er wurde Herr seines Unmuts und sagte bloß sehr ernst: »Wohl mag euch, ihr kalten prosaischen Menschen, Olimpia unheimlich sein. Nur dem poetischen Gemut entfaltet sich das gleich organisierte! Nur mir ging ihr Liebesblick auf und durchstrahlte Sinn und Gedanken, nur in Olimpias Liebe finde ich mein Selbst wieder. Euch mag es nicht recht sein, daß sie nicht in platter Konversation faselt, wie die andern flachen Gemüter. Sie spricht wenig Worte, das ist wahr; aber diese wenigen Worte erscheinen als echte Hieroglyphe der innern Welt voll Liebe und hoher Erkenntnis des geistigen Lebens in der Anschauung des ewigen Jenseits. Doch für alles das habt ihr keinen Sinn und alles sind verlorne Worte.«

"God be with you, brother," said Siegmund very gently, almost sadly, "but it seems to me that you are in a very bad way. You may rely upon me, if all—No, I can't say any more." It all at once dawned upon Nathanael that his cold prosaic friend Siegmund really and sincerely wished him well, and so he warmly shook his proffered hand.

Nathanael had completely forgotten that there was a Clara in the world, whom he had once loved—and his mother and Lothair. They had all vanished from his mind; he lived for Olimpia alone. He sat beside her every day for hours together, rhapsodising about his love and sympathy enkindled into life, and about psychic elective affinity—all of which Olimpia listened to with great reverence. He fished up from the very bottom of his desk all the things that he had ever written—poems, fancy sketches, visions, romances, tales, and the heap was increased daily with all kinds of aimless sonnets, stanzas, canzonets. All these he read to Olimpia hour after hour without growing tired; but then he had never had such an exemplary listener. She neither embroidered, nor knitted; she did not look out of the window, or feed a bird, or play with a little pet dog or a favourite cat, neither did she twist a piece of paper or anything of that kind round her finger; she did not forcibly convert a yawn into a low affected cough—in short, she sat hour after hour with her eyes bent unchangeably upon her lover's face, without moving or altering her position, and her gaze grew more ardent and more ardent still. And it was only when at last Nathanael rose and kissed her lips or her hand that she said, "Ach! Ach!" and then "Good-night, dear." Arrived in his own room, Nathanael would break out with, "Oh! what a brilliant—what a profound mind! Only you—you alone understand me." And his heart trembled with rapture when he reflected upon the wondrous harmony which daily revealed itself between his own and his Olimpia's character; for he fancied that she had expressed in respect to his works and his poetic genius the identical sentiments which he himself cherished deep down in his own heart in respect to the same, and even as if it was his own heart's voice speaking to him. And it must indeed have been so; for Olimpia never uttered any other words than those already mentioned. And when Nathanael himself in his clear and sober moments, as, for instance, directly after waking in a morning, thought about her utter passivity and taciturnity, he only said, "What are words—but words? The glance of her heavenly eyes says more than any tongue of earth. And how can, anyway, a child of heaven accustom herself to the narrow circle which the exigencies of a wretched mundane life demand?"

»Behüte dich Gott, Herr Bruder«, sagte Siegmund sehr sanft, beinahe wehmütig, »aber mir scheint es, du seist auf bösem Wege. Auf mich kannst du rechnen, wenn alles - Nein, ich mag nichts weiter sagen! -« Dem Nathanael war es plötzlich, als meine der kalte prosaische Siegmund es sehr treu mit ihm, er schüttelte daher die ihm dargebotene Hand recht herzlich.

Nathanael hatte rein vergessen, daß es eine Clara in der Welt gebe, die er sonst geliebt; - die Mutter - Lothar - alle waren aus seinem Gedächtnis entschwunden, er lebte nur für Olimpia, bei der er täglich stundenlang saß und von seiner Liebe, von zum Leben erglühter Sympathie, von psychischer Wahlverwandtschaft fantasierte, welches alles Olimpia mit großer Andacht anhörte. Aus dem tiefsten Grunde des Schreibpults holte Nathanael alles hervor, was er jemals geschrieben. Gedichte, Fantasien, Visionen, Romane, Erzählungen, das wurde täglich vermehrt mit allerlei ins Blaue fliegenden Sonetten, Stanzen, Kanzonen, und das alles las er der Olimpia stundenlang hintereinander vor, ohne zu ermüden. Aber auch noch nie hatte er eine solche herrliche Zuhörerin gehabt. Sie stickte und strickte nicht, sie sah nicht durchs Fenster, sie fütterte keinen Vogel, sie spielte mit keinem Schoßhündchen, mit keiner Lieblingskatze, sie drehte keine Papierschnitzchen, oder sonst etwas in der Hand, sie durfte kein Gähnen durch einen leisen erzwungenen Husten bezwingen - kurz! - stundenlang sah sie mit starrem Blick unverwandt dem Geliebten ins Auge, ohne sich zu rücken und zu bewegen und immer glühender, immer lebendiger wurde dieser Blick. Nur wenn Nathanael endlich aufstand und ihr die Hand, auch wohl den Mund küßte, sagte sie: »Ach, Ach!« - dann aber: »Gute Nacht, mein Lieber!« - »O du herrliches, du tiefes Gemüt«, rief Nathanael auf seiner Stube: »nur von dir, von dir allein werd ich ganz verstanden.« Er erbebte vor innerm Entzücken, wenn er bedachte, welch wunderbarer Zusammenklang sich in seinem und Olimpias Gemüt täglich mehr offenbare; denn es schien ihm, als habe Olimpia über seine Werke, über seine Dichtergabe überhaupt recht tief aus seinem Innern gesprochen, ja als habe die Stimme aus seinem Innern selbst herausgetönt. Das mußte denn wohl auch sein; denn mehr Worte als vorhin erwähnt, sprach Olimpia niemals. Erinnerte sich aber auch Nathanael in hellen nüchternen Augenblicken, z.B. morgens gleich nach dem Erwachen, wirklich an Olimpias gänzliche Passivität und Wortkargheit, so sprach er doch: »Was sind Worte - Worte! - Der Blick ihres himmlischen Auges sagt mehr als jede Sprache hienieden. Vermag denn überhaupt ein Kind des Himmels sich einzuschichten in den engen Kreis, den ein klägliches irdisches Bedürfnis gezogen?«

Professor Spalanzani appeared to be greatly pleased at the intimacy that had sprung up between his daughter Olimpia and Nathanael, and showed the young man many unmistakable proofs of his good feeling towards him; and when Nathanael ventured at length to hint very delicately at an alliance with Olimpia, the Professor smiled all over his face at once, and said he should allow his daughter to make a perfectly free choice. Encouraged by these words, and with the fire of desire burning in his heart, Nathanael resolved the very next day to implore Olimpia to tell him frankly, in plain words, what he had long read in her sweet loving glances,—that she would be his for ever. He looked for the ring which his mother had given him at parting; he would present it to Olimpia as a symbol of his devotion, and of the happy life he was to lead with her from that time onwards. Whilst looking for it he came across his letters from Clara and Lothair; he threw them carelessly aside, found the ring, put it in his pocket, and ran across to Olimpia. Whilst still on the stairs, in the entrance-passage, he heard an extraordinary hubbub; the noise seemed to proceed from Spalanzani's study. There was a stamping—a rattling—pushing—knocking against the door, with curses and oaths intermingled. "Leave hold—leave hold—you monster—you rascal—staked your life and honour upon it?—Ha! ha! ha! ha!—That was not our wager—I, I made the eyes—I the clock-work.—Go to the devil with your clock-work—you damned dog of a watch-maker—be off—Satan—stop—you paltry turner—you infernal beast!—stop—begone—let me go." The voices which were thus making all this racket and rumpus were those of Spalanzani and the fearsome Coppelius. Nathanael rushed in, impelled by some nameless dread. The Professor was grasping a female figure by the shoulders, the Italian Coppola held her by the feet; and they were pulling and dragging each other backwards and forwards, fighting furiously to get possession of her. Nathanael recoiled with horror on recognising that the figure was Olimpia. Boiling with rage, he was about to tear his beloved from the grasp of the madmen, when Coppola by an extraordinary exertion of strength twisted the figure out of the Professor's hands and gave him such a terrible blow with her, that he reeled backwards and fell over the table all amongst the phials and retorts, the bottles and glass cylinders, which covered it: all these things were smashed into a thousand pieces. But Coppola threw the figure across his shoulder, and, laughing shrilly and horribly, ran hastily down the stairs, the figure's ugly feet hanging down and banging and rattling like wood against the steps. Nathanael was stupefied;—he had seen only too distinctly that in Olimpia's pallid waxed face there were no eyes, merely black holes in their stead; she was an inanimate puppet. Spalanzani was rolling on the floor; the pieces of glass had cut his head and breast and arm; the blood was escaping from him in streams. But he gathered his strength together by an effort.

Professor Spalanzani schien hocherfreut über das Verhältnis seiner Tochter mit Nathanael; er gab diesem allerlei unzweideutige Zeichen seines Wohlwollens und als es Nathanael endlich wagte von ferne auf eine Verbindung mit Olimpia anzuspielen, lächelte dieser mit dem ganzen Gesicht und meinte: er werde seiner Tochter völlig freie Wahl lassen. - Ermutigt durch diese Worte, brennendes Verlangen im Herzen, beschloß Nathanael, gleich am folgenden Tage Olimpia anzusehen, daß sie das unumwunden in deutlichen Worten ausspreche, was längst ihr holder Liebesblick ihm gesagt, daß sie sein eigen immerdar sein wolle. Er suchte nach dem Ringe, den ihm beim Abschiede die Mutter geschenkt, um ihn Olimpia als Symbol seiner Hingebung, seines mit ihr aufkeimenden, blühenden Lebens darzureichen. Claras, Lothars Briefe fielen ihm dabei in die Hände; gleichgültig warf er sie beiseite, fand den Ring, steckte ihn ein und rannte herüber zu Olimpia. Schon auf der Treppe, auf dem Flur, vernahm er ein wunderliches Getöse; es schien aus Spalanzanis Studierzimmer herauszuschallen. - Ein Stampfen - ein Klirren - ein Stoßen - Schlagen gegen die Tür, dazwischen Flüche und Verwünschungen. Laß los - laß los - Infamer - Verruchter! - Darum Leib und Leben daran gesetzt? - ha ha ha ha! - so haben wir nicht gewettet - ich, ich hab die Augen gemacht - ich das Räderwerk - dummer Teufel mit deinem Räderwerk - verfluchter Hund von einfältigem Uhrmacher - fort mit dir - Satan - halt - Peipendreher - teuflische Bestie! - halt - fort - laß los! - Es waren Spalanzanis und des gräßlichen Coppelius Stimmen, die so durcheinander schwirrten und tobten. Hinein stürzte Nathanael von namenloser Angst ergriffen. Der Professor hatte eine weibliche Figur bei den Schultern gepackt, der Italiener Coppola bei den Füßen, die zerrten und zogen sie hin und her, streitend in voller Wut um den Besitz. Voll tiefen Entsetzens prallte Nathanael zurück, als er die Figur für Olimpia erkannte; aufflammend in wildem Zorn wollte er den Wütenden die Geliebte entreißen, aber in dem Augenblick wand Coppola sich mit Riesenkraft drehend die Figur dem Professor aus den Händen und versetzte ihm mit der Figur selbst einen fürchterlichen Schlag, daß er rücklings über den Tisch, auf dem Phiolen, Retorten, Flaschen, gläserne Zylinder standen, taumelte und hinstürzte; alles Gerät klirrte in tausend Scherben zusammen. Nun warf Coppola die Figur über die Schulter und rannte mit fürchterlich gellendem Gelächter rasch fort die Treppe herab, so daß die häßlich herunterhängenden Füße der Figur auf den Stufen hölzern klapperten und dröhnten. - Erstarrt stand Nathanael - nur zu deutlich hatte er gesehen, Olimpias toderbleiches Wachsgesicht hatte keine Augen, statt ihrer schwarze Höhlen; sie war eine leblose Puppe. Spalanzani wälzte sich auf der Erde, Glasscherben hatten ihm Kopf, Brust und Arm zerschnitten, wie aus Springquellen strömte das Blut empor. Aber er raffte seine Kräfte zusammen.

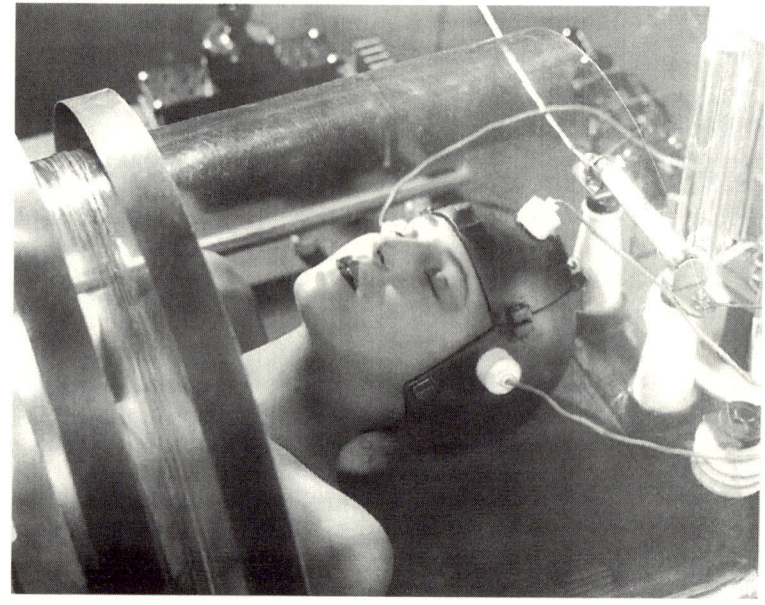

Metropolis (1927)

Elegy—Elegie by Christian Rohlfs (c. 1898)

"After him—after him! What do you stand staring there for? Coppelius—Coppelius—he's stolen my best automaton—at which I've worked for twenty years—staked my life upon it—the clock-work— speech—movement—mine—your eyes—stolen your eyes—damn him—curse him—after him—fetch me back Olimpia—there are the eyes." And now Nathanael saw a pair of bloody eyes lying on the floor staring at him; Spalanzani seized them with his uninjured hand and threw them at him, so that they hit his breast Then madness dug her burning talons into him and swept down into his heart, rending his mind and thoughts to shreds. "Aha! aha! aha! Fire-wheel—fire-wheel! Spin round, fire-wheel! merrily, merrily! Aha! wooden doll! spin round, pretty wooden doll!" and he threw himself upon the Professor, clutching him fast by the throat. He would certainly have strangled him had not several people, attracted by the noise, rushed in and torn away the madman; and so they saved the Professor, whose wounds were immediately dressed. Siegmund, with all his strength, was not able to subdue the frantic lunatic, who continued to scream in a dreadful way, "Spin round, wooden doll!" and to strike out right and left with his doubled fists. At length the united strength of several succeeded in overpowering him by throwing him on the floor and binding him. His cries passed into a brutish bellow that was awful to hear; and thus raging with the harrowing violence of madness, he was taken away to the madhouse.

Before continuing my narration of what happened further to the unfortunate Nathanael, I will tell you, indulgent reader, in case you take any interest in that skilful mechanician and fabricator of automata, Spalanzani, that he recovered completely from his wounds. He had, however, to leave the university, for Nathanael's fate had created a great sensation; and the opinion was pretty generally expressed that it was an imposture altogether unpardonable to have smuggled a wooden puppet instead of a living person into intelligent tea-circles,—for Olimpia had been present at several with success. Lawyers called it a cunning piece of knavery, and all the harder to punish since it was directed against the public; and it had been so craftily contrived that it had escaped unobserved by all except a few preternaturally acute students, although everybody was very wise now and remembered to have thought of several facts which occurred to them as suspicious. But these latter could not succeed in making out any sort of a consistent tale. For was it, for instance, a thing likely to occur to any one as suspicious that, according to the declaration of an elegant beau of these tea-parties, Olimpia had, contrary to all good manners, sneezed oftener than she had yawned? The former must have been, in the opinion of this elegant gentleman, the winding up of the concealed clock-work; it had always been accompanied by an observable creaking, and so on. The Professor of Poetry and Eloquence took a pinch of snuff, and, slapping the lid to and clearing his throat, said solemnly, "My most honourable ladies and gentlemen, don't you see then where the rub is? The whole thing is an allegory, a continuous metaphor. You understand me? *Sapienti sat.*"

»Ihm nach - ihm nach, was zauderst du? - Coppelius - Coppelius, mein bestes Automat hat er mir geraubt - Zwanzig Jahre daran gearbeitet - Leib und Leben daran gesetzt - das Räderwerk - Sprache - Gang - mein - die Augen - die Augen dir gestohlen. - Verdammter - Verfluchter - ihm nach - hol mir Olimpia - da hast du die Augen! -« Nun sah Nathanael, wie ein Paar blutige Augen auf dem Boden liegend ihn anstarrten, die ergriff Spalanzani mit der unverletzten Hand und warf sie nach ihm, daß sie seine Brust trafen. - Da packte ihn der Wahnsinn mit glühenden Krallen und fuhr in sein Inneres hinein Sinn und Gedanken zerreißend. »Hui - hui - hui! - Feuerkreis - Feuerkreis! dreh dich Feuerkreis - lustig - lustig! - Holzpüppchen hui schön Holzpüppchen dreh dich -« damit warf er sich auf den Professor und drückte ihm die Kehle zu. Er hätte ihn erwürgt, aber das Getöse hatte viele Menschen herbeigelockt, die drangen ein, rissen den wütenden Nathanael auf und retteten so den Professor, der gleich verbunden wurde. Siegmund, so stark er war, vermochte nicht den Rasenden zu bändigen; der schrie mit fürchterlicher Stimme immerfort: »Holzpüppchen dreh dich« und schlug um sich mit geballten Fäusten. Endlich gelang es der vereinten Kraft mehrerer, ihn zu überwältigen, indem sie ihn zu Boden warfen und banden. Seine Worte gingen unter in entsetzlichem ti- erischen Gebrüll. So in gräßlicher Raserei tobend wurde er nach dem Tollhause gebracht.

Ehe ich, günstiger Leser! dir zu erzählen fortfahre, was sich weiter mit dem unglücklichen Nathanael zugetragen, kann ich dir, solltest du einigen Anteil an dem geschickten Mechanikus und Automat-Fabrikanten Spalanzani nehmen, versichern, daß er von seinen Wunden völlig geheilt wurde. Er mußte indes die Universität verlassen, weil Nathanaels Geschichte Aufsehen erregt hatte und es allgemein für gänzlich unerlaubten Betrug gehalten wurde, vernünftigen Teezirkeln (Olimpia hatte sie mit Glück besucht) statt der lebendigen Person eine Holzpuppe einzuschwärzen. Juristen nannten es sogar einen feinen und um so härter zu bestrafenden Betrug, als er gegen das Publikum gerichtet und so schlau angelegt worden, daß kein Mensch (ganz kluge Studenten ausgenommen) es gemerkt habe, unerachtet jetzt alle weise tun und sich auf allerlei Tatsachen berufen wollten, die ihnen verdächtig vorgekommen. Diese letzteren brachten aber eigentlich nichts Gescheutes zutage. Denn konnte z.B. wohl irgend jemanden verdächtig vorgekommen sein, daß nach der Aussage eines eleganten Teeisten Olimpia gegen alle Sitte öfter genieset, als gegähnt hatte? Ersteres, meinte der Elegant, sei das Selbstaufziehen des verborgenen Triebwerks gewesen, merklich habe es dabei geknarrt usw. Der Professor der Poesie und Beredsamkeit nahm eine Prise, klappte die Dose zu, räusperte sich und sprach feierlich: »Hochzuverehrende Herren und Damen! merken Sie denn nicht, wo der Hase im Pfeffer liegt? Das Ganze ist eine Allegorie - eine fortgeführte Metapher! - Sie verstehen mich! - *Sapienti sat!*«

But several most honourable gentlemen did not rest satisfied with this explanation; the history of this automaton had sunk deeply into their souls, and an absurd mistrust of human figures began to prevail. Several lovers, in order to be fully convinced that they were not paying court to a wooden puppet, required that their mistress should sing and dance a little out of time, should embroider or knit or play with her little pug, &c., when being read to, but above all things else that she should do something more than merely listen—that she should frequently speak in such a way as to really show that her words presupposed as a condition some thinking and feeling. The bonds of love were in many cases drawn closer in consequence, and so of course became more engaging; in other instances they gradually relaxed and fell away. "I cannot really be made responsible for it," was the remark of more than one young gallant. At the tea-gatherings everybody, in order to ward off suspicion, yawned to an incredible extent and never sneezed. Spalanzani was obliged, as has been said, to leave the place in order to escape a criminal charge of having fraudulently imposed an automaton upon human society. Coppola, too, had also disappeared.

When Nathanael awoke he felt as if he had been oppressed by a terrible nightmare; he opened his eyes and experienced an indescribable sensation of mental comfort, whilst a soft and most beautiful sensation of warmth pervaded his body. He lay on his own bed in his own room at home; Clara was bending over him, and at a little distance stood his mother and Lothair. "At last, at last, O my darling Nathanael; now we have you again; now you are cured of your grievous illness, now you are mine again." And Clara's words came from the depths of her heart; and she clasped him in her arms. The bright scalding tears streamed from his eyes, he was so overcome with mingled feelings of sorrow and delight; and he gasped forth, "My Clara, my Clara!" Siegmund, who had staunchly stood by his friend in his hour of need, now came into the room. Nathanael gave him his hand—"My faithful brother, you have not deserted me." Every trace of insanity had left him, and in the tender hands of his mother and his beloved, and his friends, he quickly recovered his strength again. Good fortune had in the meantime visited the house; a niggardly old uncle, from whom they had never expected to get anything, had died, and left Nathanael's mother not only a considerable fortune, but also a small estate, pleasantly situated not far from the town. There they resolved to go and live, Nathanael and his mother, and Clara, to whom he was now to be married, and Lothair. Nathanael was become gentler and more childlike than he had ever been before, and now began really to understand Clara's supremely pure and noble character. None of them ever reminded him, even in the remotest degree, of the past. But when Siegmund took leave of him, he said, "By heaven, brother! I was in a bad way, but an angel came just at the right moment and led me back upon the path of light. Yes, it was Clara." Siegmund would not let him speak further, fearing lest the painful recollections of the past might arise too vividly and too intensely in his mind.

Aber viele hochzuverehrende Herren beruhigten sich nicht dabei; die Geschichte mit dem Automat hatte tief in ihrer Seele Wurzel gefaßt und es schlich sich in der Tat abscheuliches Mißtrauen gegen menschliche Figuren ein. Um nun ganz überzeugt zu werden, daß man keine Holzpuppe liebe, wurde von mehrern Liebhabern verlangt, daß die Geliebte etwas taktlos singe und tanze, daß sie beim Vorlesen sticke, stricke, mit dem Möpschen spiele usw. vor allen Dingen aber, daß sie nicht bloß höre, sondern auch manchmal in der Art spreche, daß dies Sprechen wirklich ein Denken und Empfinden voraussetze. Das Liebesbündnis vieler wurde fester und dabei anmutiger, andere dagegen gingen leise auseinander. »Man kann wahrhaftig nicht dafür stehen«, sagte dieser und jener. In den Tees wurde unglaublich gegähnt und niemals genieset, um jedem Verdacht zu begegnen. - Spalanzani mußte, wie gesagt, fort, um der Kriminaluntersuchung wegen [des] der menschlichen Gesellschaft betrüglicherweise eingeschobenen Automats zu entgehen. Coppola war auch verschwunden.

Nathanael erwachte wie aus schwerem, fürchterlichem Traum, er schlug die Augen auf und fühlte wie ein unbeschreibliches Wonnegefühl mit sanfter himmlischer Wärme ihn durchströmte. Er lag in seinem Zimmer in des Vaters Hause auf dem Bette, Clara hatte sich über ihn hingebeugt und unfern standen die Mutter und Lothar. »Endlich, endlich, o mein herzlieber Nathanael - nun bist du genesen von schwerer Krankheit - nun bist du wieder mein!« - So sprach Clara recht aus tiefer Seele und faßte den Nathanael in ihre Arme. Aber dem quollen vor lauter Wehmut und Entzücken die hellen glühenden Tränen aus den Augen und er stöhnte tief auf. »Meine - meine Clara!« - Siegmund, der getreulich ausgeharrt bei dem Freunde in großer Not, trat herein. Nathanael reichte ihm die Hand: »Du treuer Bruder hast mich doch nicht verlassen.« - Jede Spur des Wahnsinns war verschwunden, bald erkräftigte sich Nathanael in der sorglichen Pflege der Mutter, der Geliebten, der Freunde. Das Glück war unterdessen in das Haus eingekehrt; denn ein alter karger Oheim, von dem niemand etwas gehofft, war gestorben und hatte der Mutter nebst einem nicht unbedeutenden Vermögen ein Gütchen in einer angenehmen Gegend unfern der Stadt hinterlassen. Dort wollten sie hinziehen, die Mutter, Nathanael mit seiner Clara, die er nun zu heiraten gedachte, und Lothar. Nathanael war milder, kindlicher geworden, als er je gewesen und erkannte nun erst recht Claras himmlisch reines, herrliches Gemüt. Niemand erinnerte ihn auch nur durch den leisesten Anklang an die Vergangenheit. Nur, als Siegmund von ihm schied, sprach Nathanael: »Bei Gott Bruder! ich war auf schlimmen Wege, aber zu rechter Zeit leitete mich ein Engel auf den lichten Pfad! - Ach es war ja Clara! -« Siegmund ließ ihn nicht weiter reden, aus Besorgnis, tief verletzende Erinnerungen möchten ihm zu hell und flammend aufgehen.

The time came for the four happy people to move to their little property. At noon they were going through the streets. After making several purchases they found that the lofty tower of the town-house was throwing its giant shadows across the market-place. "Come," said Clara, "let us go up to the top once more and have a look at the distant hills." No sooner said than done. Both of them, Nathanael and Clara, went up the tower; their mother, however, went on with the servant-girl to her new home, and Lothair, not feeling inclined to climb up all the many steps, waited below. There the two lovers stood arm-in-arm on the topmost gallery of the tower, and gazed out into the sweet-scented wooded landscape, beyond which the blue hills rose up like a giant's city.

"Oh! do look at that strange little grey bush, it looks as if it were actually walking towards us," said Clara. Mechanically he put his hand into his sidepocket; he found Coppola's perspective and looked for the bush; Clara stood in front of the glass. Then a convulsive thrill shot through his pulse and veins; pale as a corpse, he fixed his staring eyes upon her; but soon they began to roll, and a fiery current flashed and sparkled in them, and he yelled fearfully, like a hunted animal. Leaping up high in the air and laughing horribly at the same time, he began to shout, in a piercing voice, "Spin round, wooden doll! Spin round, wooden doll!" With the strength of a giant he laid hold upon Clara and tried to hurl her over, but in an agony of despair she clutched fast hold of the railing that went round the gallery. Lothair heard the madman raging and Clara's scream of terror: a fearful presentiment flashed across his mind. He ran up the steps; the door of the second flight was locked. Clara's scream for help rang out more loudly. Mad with rage and fear, he threw himself against the door, which at length gave way. Clara's cries were growing fainter and fainter,— "Help! save me! save me!" and her voice died away in the air. "She is killed— murdered by that madman," shouted Lothair. The door to the gallery was also locked. Despair gave him the strength of a giant; he burst the door off its hinges. Good God! there was Clara in the grasp of the madman Nathanael, hanging over the gallery in the air; she only held to the iron bar with one hand. Quick as lightning, Lothair seized his sister and pulled her back, at the same time dealing the madman a blow in the face with his doubled fist, which sent him reeling backwards, forcing him to let go his victim.

Lothair ran down with his insensible sister in his arms. She was saved. But Nathanael ran round and round the gallery, leaping up in the air and shouting, "Spin round, fire-wheel! Spin round, fire-wheel!" The people heard the wild shouting, and a crowd began to gather. In the midst of them towered the advocate Coppelius, like a giant; he had only just arrived in the town, and had gone straight to the market-place. Some were going up to overpower and take charge of the madman, but Coppelius laughed and said, "Ha! ha! wait a bit; he'll come down of his own accord;" and he stood gazing upwards along with the rest. All at once Nathanael stopped as if spell-bound; he bent down over the railing, and perceived Coppelius. With a piercing scream, "Ha! foine oyes! foine oyes!" he leapt over.

Es war an der Zeit, daß die vier glücklichen Menschen nach dem Gütchen ziehen wollten. Zur Mittagsstunde gingen sie durch die Straßen der Stadt. Sie hatten manches eingekauft, der hohe Ratsturm warf seinen Riesenschatten über den Markt. »Ei!« sagte Clara: »steigen wir doch noch einmal herauf und schauen in das ferne Gebirge hinein!« Gesagt, getan! Beide, Nathanael und Clara, stiegen herauf, die Mutter ging mit der Dienstmagd nach Hause, und Lothar, nicht geneigt, die vielen Stufen zu erklettern, wollte unten warten. Da standen die beiden Liebenden Arm in Arm auf der höchsten Galerie des Turmes und schauten hinein in die duftigen Waldungen, hinter denen das blaue Gebirge, wie eine Riesenstadt, sich erhob.

»Sieh doch den sonderbaren kleinen grauen Busch, der ordentlich auf uns los zu schreiten scheint«, frug Clara. - Nathanael faßte mechanisch nach der Seitentasche; er fand Coppolas Perspektiv, er schaute seitwärts - Clara stand vor dem Glase! - Da zuckte es krampfhaft in seinen Pulsen und Adern - totenbleich starrte er Clara an, aber bald glühten und sprühten Feuerströme durch die rollenden Augen, gräßlich brüllte er auf, wie ein gehetztes Tier; dann sprang er hoch in die Lüfte und grausig dazwischen lachend schrie er in schneidendem Ton: »Holzpüppchen dreh dich - Holzpüppchen dreh dich« - und mit gewaltiger Kraft faßte er Clara und wollte sie herabschleudern, aber Clara krallte sich in verzweifelnder Todesangst fest an das Geländer. Lothar hörte den Rasenden toben, er hörte Claras Angstgeschrei, gräßliche Ahnung durchflog ihn, er rannte herauf, die Tür der zweiten Treppe war verschlossen - stärker hallte Claras Jammergeschrei. Unsinnig vor Wut und Angst stieß er gegen die Tür, die endlich aufsprang - Matter und matter wurden nun Claras Laute: »Hülfe - rettet - rettet -« so erstarb die Stimme in den Lüften. »Sie ist hin - ermordet von dem Rasenden«, so schrie Lothar. Auch die Tür zur Galerie war zugeschlagen. - Die Verzweiflung gab ihm Riesenkraft, er sprengte die Tür aus den Angeln. Gott im Himmel - Clara schwebte von dem rasenden Nathanael erfaßt über der Galerie in den Lüften - nur mit einer Hand hatte sie noch die Eisenstäbe umklammert. Rasch wie der Blitz erfaßte Lothar die Schwester, zog sie hinein, und schlug im demselben Augenblick mit geballter Faust dem Wütenden ins Gesicht, daß er zurückprallte und die Todesbeute fallen ließ.

Lothar rannte herab, die ohnmächtige Schwester in den Armen. - Sie war gerettet. - Nun raste Nathanael herum auf der Galerie und sprang hoch in die Lüfte und schrie »Feuerkreis dreh dich - Feuerkreis dreh dich« - Die Menschen liefen auf das wilde Geschrei zusammen; unter ihnen ragte riesengroß der Advokat Coppelius hervor, der eben in die Stadt gekommen und gerades Weges nach dem Markt geschritten war. Man wollte herauf, um sich des Rasenden zu bemächtigen, da lachte Coppelius sprechend: »Ha ha - wartet nur, der kommt schon herunter von selbst«, und schaute wie die übrigen hinauf. Nathanael blieb plötzlich wie erstarrt stehen, er bückte sich herab, wurde den Coppelius gewahr und mit dem gellenden Schrei: »Ha! Sköne Oke - Sköne Oke«, sprang er über das Geländer.

When Nathanael lay on the stone pavement with a broken head, Coppelius had disappeared in the crush and confusion.

Several years afterwards it was reported that, outside the door of a pretty country house in a remote district, Clara had been seen sitting hand in hand with a pleasant gentleman, whilst two bright boys were playing at her feet. From this it may be concluded that she eventually found that quiet domestic happiness which her cheerful, blithesome character required, and which Nathanael, with his tempest-tossed soul, could never have been able to give her.

Als Nathanael mit zerschmettertem Kopf auf dem, Steinpflaster lag, war Coppelius im Gewühl verschwunden.

Nach mehreren Jahren will man in einer entfernten Gegend Clara gesehen haben, wie sie mit einem freundlichen Mann, Hand in Hand vor der Türe eines schönen Landhauses saß und vor ihr zwei muntre Knaben spielten. Es wäre daraus zu schließen, daß Clara das ruhige häusliche Glück noch fand, das ihrem heitern lebenslustigen Sinn zusagte und das ihr der im Innern zerrissene Nathanael niemals hätte gewähren können.

Scenes from *The Tales of Hoffmann* from the Paris premiere (1881)

Act II

(A physician's room, richly furnished.)

HOFFMAN *(alone)*

Come! Courage and confidence;
I become a well of science.
I must turn with the wind that blows,
To deserve the one I love.
I shall know how to find in myself
The stuff of a learned man.
She is there... if I dared.

(He softly lifts the portiere.)

    'Tis she!
She sleeps... how beautiful!
Ah! together live... both in the same hope,
The same remembrance
Divide our happiness and our sorrow,
And share the future.
Let, let my flame
Pour in thee the light,
Let your soul but open
To the rays of Love.
Divine hearth! Sun whose ardor penetrates
And comes to kiss us.
Ineffable desire where one's whole being
Melts in a single kiss.
Let, let my flame,
etc., etc.

(Nicklausse appears.)

NICKLAUSSE

By Jove, I felt sure you'd be here.

Acte II

(*Un riche cabinet de physician.*)

HOFFMANN (*seul*).

Allons courage et confiance
Je deviens un puit de science
Il faut tourner selon le vent
Pour meriter celle que j'aime.
Je saurai trouver en moi-même
L'étoffe d'un savant
Elle est là, si j'osais.

(*Il soulève la portière.*)

    C'est elle!
Elle sommeille! Qu'elle est belle!
Ah! vivre deux! N'avoir qu'une même espérance
Un même souvenir!
Partager le bonheur, partager la souffrance,
Partager l'avenir!
Laisse, laisse ma flamme
Verser en toi le jour!
Laisse éclore ton âme
Aux rayons de l'amour!
Foyer divin! Soleil dont l'ardeur nous penêtre
Et nous vient embraser!
Ineffable désir ou l'on sent tout son être
Se fondre en un baiser.
Laisse, laisse ma flamme
Verser en toi le jour!
Laisse éclore ton âme
Aux rayons de l'amour!
Foyer divin! Soleil dont l'ardeur nous pénêtre,
Et nous vient embraser!
Ineffable désir où l'on sent tout son être
Se fondre en un baiser.
Laisse laisse ma flamme
Verser en toi le jour!
Laisse éclore ton âme
Aux rayons de l'amour!

(*NICKLAUSSE parait.*)

NICKLAUSSE

Pardieu... j'étais bien sur de te trouver ici!

Hoffmann (tenor Gerard Powers) captivates tavern patrons
with his story telling.

Wolfram (bass Bradley Smoak), Nicklausse (mezzo-soprano Michéle Losier),
Maître Luther (baritone Ulysses Thomas) and Mrs. Luther (Lee O'Connell)
listen closely as Hoffmann (tenor Gerard Powers) reflects upon a lost love.

HOFFMAN (*letting portiere fall*)

Chut.

NICKLAUSSE

Why? 'tis there that breathes
The dove who's now your amorous care,
The beautiful Olympia? Go, my child, admire!

HOFFMANN

Yes, I adore her!

NICKLAUSSE

Want to know her better.

HOFFMANN

The soul one loves is easy to know.

NICKLAUSSE

What? by a look... through a window?

HOFFMANN

A look is enough to embrace the heavens.

NICKLAUSSE

What warmth!... At least she knows that you love her.

HOFFMANN

No.

NICKLAUSSE

Write her.

HOFFMANN

I don't dare.

NICKLAUSSE

Poor lamb! Speak to her.

HOFFMANN

The dangers are the same.

NICKLAUSSE

Then sing, to get out of the scrape.

HOFFMANN

Monsieur Spalanzani doesn't like music.

HOFFMANN (*laissant retomber la portière*).

Chut!

NICKLAUSSE

Pourquoi?... c'est là que respire
La colombe qui fait ton amoureux souci.
La belle Olympia... Va, mon enfant! admire!

HOFFMANN

Oui, je l'adore!

NICKLAUSSE

Attends à la connaître mieux.

HOFFMANN

L'âme qu'on aime est aisé a connaître!

NICKLAUSSE

Quoi d'un regard?... par la fenêtre?

HOFFMANN

Il suffit d'un regard pour embrasser les cieux!

NICKLAUSSE

Qu'elle chaleur! Au moins sait—elle que tu l'aimes?

HOFFMANN

Non!

NICKLAUSSE

Ecris lui!

HOFFMANN

Je n'ose pas.

NICKLAUSSE

Pauvre agneau! Parle-lui.

HOFFMANN

Les dangers sont les mêmes.

NICKLAUSSE

Alors chante morbleu! pour sortir d'un tel pas!

HOFFMANN

Monsieur Spalanzani n'aime pas la musique.

NICKLAUSSE (*laughing*).

Yes, I know, all for physics!
A doll with china eyes
Nearby a little cock in brass;
Both sang in unison
In a marvelous way,
Danced, gossiped, seemed to live.

HOFFMANN

Beg your pardon. Why this song?

NICKLAUSSE

The little cock shining and smart,
With a very knowing air,
Three times on himself turned;
By some ingenious wheels,
The doll in rolling its eyes
Sighed and said: "I love you."

CHORUS OF THE INVITED GUESTS

No, no host, really,
Receives more richly
Through good taste his house shines;
Everything here matches.
No, no host really
Receives more richly.

SPALANZANI

You will be satisfied, gentlemen, in a moment.

(*He makes sign to Cochenille to follow him and exits with him.*)

NICKLAUSSE (*to HOFFMANN*).

At last we shall more nearly see this marvel
Without equal!

HOFFMANN

Silence... she is here!

(*Enter SPALANZANI conducting OLYMPIA.*)

SPALANZANI

Ladies and gentlemen,
I present to you
My daughter Olympia.

NICKLAUSSE (*riant*).

Oui, je sais, tout pour le physique!
Une poupée aux yeux d'email
Jouait au mieux de l'eventail
Aupres d'un petit coq en cuire;
Tous deux chantaient a l'unison
D'une merveilleuse facon,
Dansaient, caquetaient, semblaient vivre.

HOFFMANN

Plait-il? Pourquoi cette chanson?

NICKLAUSSE

Le petit coq luisant et vif,
Avec un air rèbarbatif,
Tournait par trois sur lui-même;
Par un rouage ingenieux,
La poupée, en roulant les yeux
Soupirait et disait: "Je t'aime"!
Le Choeur des Invites.
Non, aucun hôte, vraiment,
Ne recoit plus richement!
Par le gout, sa maison brille!
Tout s'y trouve réuni.

SPALANZANI

Vous serez satisfaits, messieurs.

(*Il fait signe a COCHENILLE et sort.*)

NICKLAUSSE (*a HOFFMANN*).

Enfin nous allons voir de près cette merveille.
Sans pareille!

HOFFMANN

Silence! la voici.

(*Entrée de SPALANZANI conduisant OLYMPIA.*)

SPALANZANI

Mesdames et messieurs je vous présente

Ma fille Olympia.

THE CHORUS

Charming.
She has beautiful eyes!
Her shape is very good!
See how well apparelled!
Nothing is wanting!
She does very well!

HOFFMANN

Ah, how adorable she is!

NICKLAUSSE

Charming, incomparable!

SPALANZANI (*to Olympia*).

What a success is thine!

NICKLAUSSE (*taking her all in*).

Really she does very well.

THE CHORUS

She has beautiful eyes,
Her shape is very good,
See how well apparelled,
Nothing is really wanting;
She does very well.

SPALANZANI

Ladies and gentlemen, proud of your applause,
And above all anxious
To conquer more,
My daughter obedient to your least caprice
Will, if you please...

NICKLAUSSE (*aside*).

Pass to other exercises.

SPALANZANI

Sing to a grand air, following with the voice,
Rare talent
The clavichord, the guitar,
Or the harp, at your choice!

COCHENILLE (*at the rear*).

The harp!

LE CHOEUR

Charmante!
Elle à de trés beauv yeaux!
Sa taille est fort bien prise!
Voyez comme elle est mise!
Il ne lui manque rien!
Elle est très bien!

HOFFMANN

Ah qu'elle est adorable!

NICKLAUSSE

Charmante, incomparable!

SPALANZANI (*a OLYMPIA*).

Quel succès est le tien.

NICKLAUSSE

Vraiment elle est très bien.

LE CHOEUR

Elle à de beaux yeux
Sa taille est fort bien prise
Voyez comme elle est mise
Il ne lui manque rien
Vraiment elle est très bien.

SPALANZANI

Mesdames et messieurs, fière de vos bravos.
Et surtont impatiente
D'en conquerir de nonveaux
Ma fille, obéissant à vos moindres caprices,
Va, s'il vous plait...

NICKLAUSSE (*à part*).

Passer a d'autres exercices.

SPALANZANI

Vous chanter un grand air, en suivant de la voix,
Talent rare
Le clavecin, la guitare,
Qu la harpe, à votre choix!

COCHENILLE (*au fond du théâtre*).

La harpe!

BASS VOICE (*in the wings*).

The harp!

SPALANZANI

Very good, Cochenille!
Go quickly and bring my daughter's harp!

(*COCHENILLE exits*).

HOFFMANN (*aside*).

I shall hear her... oh joy!

NICKLAUSSE (*aside*).

Oh, crazy passion!

SPALANZANI (*to OLYMPIA*).

Master your emotion, my child!

OLYMPIA

Yes.

COCHENILLE (*bringing the harp*).

There!

SPALANZANI (*sitting beside OLYMPIA*).

Gentlemen, attention!

COCHENILLE

Attention!

THE CHORUS

Attention!

OLYMPIA (*accompanied by SPALANZANI*)

The birds in the bushes.
In the heavens the orb of day,
All speaks to the young girl
Of love, of love!
There!
The pretty song,
There!
The song of Olympia,
Ha!

THE CHORUS

'Tis the song of Olympia!

UNE VOIX DE BASSE (*Dans la coulisse.*)

La harpe!

SPALANZANI

Fort bien. Cochenille!
Va vite nous chercher la harpe de ma fille!

(*COCHENILLE sort.*)

HOFFMANN (*a part*).

Je vais l'entendre... oh joie!

NICKLAUSSE (*a part*).

O folle passion!

SPALANZANI (*a OLYMPIA*).

Maitrise ton émotion, mon enfant!

OLYMPIA.

Oui.

COCHENILLE (*avec la harpe*).

Voila!

SPALANZANI (*s'asseyant ouprès d'OLYMPIA*).

Messieurs, attention!

COCHENILLE

Attention!

LE CHOEUR.

Attention!

OLYMPIA (*accompagné par SPALANZANI*).

Les oiseaux dans la charmille,
Dans les cieux l'astre du jour,
Tout parle a la jeune fille
D'amour, d'amour,
Voilà!
La chanson gentille
Voilà!
La chason d'Olympia,
Ha!

LE CHOEUR.

C'est la chanson d'OLYMPIA!

The scientist Spalanzani (tenor Neal Ferreira) strikes an unlikely deal with the nefarious inventor Coppélius (baritone Gaétan Laperrière).

The scientist Spalanzani (tenor Neal Ferreira) shows off his prize creation, the singing and dancing automaton, Olympia (soprano Georgia Jarman).

OLYMPIA

All that sings and resounds
Has its sighs in turn,
Moves its heart that trembles
With love.
There.
The little song,
There, there,
The song of Olympia,
Ha!

Chorus.

'Tis the song of OLYMPIA.

HOFFMANN (*to NICKLAUSSE*)

Ah, my friend, what an accent.

NICKLAUSSE

What runs!

(*COCHENILLE has taken the harp and all surround OLYMPIA. A servant speaks to SPALANZANI*)

Come gentlemen! your arm to the ladies.
Supper awaits you!

THE CHORUS

Supper! That's good...

SPALANZANI

Unless you would prefer
To dance first.

THE CHORUS (*with energy*)

No! no! the supper... good thing...
After we'll dance.

SPALANZANI

As you please...

HOFFMANN (*approaching OLYMPIA*)

Might I dare...

SPALANZANI (*interrupting*)

She is a bit tired,
Wait for the ball.

OLYMPIA.

Tout ce qui chante et résonne
Et soupire tour à tour,
Emeut son coeur qui frissonne
D'amour!
Voilà!
La chanson mignonne
Violà voilà
La chanson d'Olympia.
Ha!

LE CHOEUR.

C'est la chanson d'OLYMPIA.

HOFFMANN (*a NICKLAUSSE*).

Ah! mon ami, quel accent.

NICKLAUSSE

Quelles gammes!...

(*Tout le monde s'empresse autour d'OLYMPIA. Un laquais s'address a SPALANZANI*).

SPALANZANI

Allons, messieurs! la main aux dames...
Le souper nous attend.

LE CHOEUR.

Le souper! bon cela...

SPALANZANI

A moins qu'on ne préfère.
Danser d'abord!...

LE CHOEUR (*avec energie*).

Non, non, le souper! bonne affaire ensuite on dansera.

SPALANZANI

Comme il vous plaira!

HOFFMANN (*s'approchant d'OLYMPIA*).

Oserai-je?

SPALANZANI (*intervenant*).

Elle est un peu lasse; attendez le bal.

(He touches OLYMPIA's shoulder.)

OLYMPIA

Yes.

SPALANZANI

You see. Until then
Will you do me the favor
To keep company with my Olympia?

HOFFMANN

Oh happiness!

SPALANZANI *(aside, laughing)*

We'll see what kind a story he'll give her.

NICKLAUSSE *(to SPALANZANI)*

Won't she take supper?

SPALANZANI

No.

NICKLAUSSE *(aside)*

Poetic soul!

(SPALANZANI goes behind OLYMPIA. Noise of a spring is heard. NICKLAUSSE turns around.)

What did you say?

SPALANZANI

Nothing, physics! ah, monsieur, physics!

(He conducts OLYMPIA to a chair. Goes out with guests)

COCHENILLE

The supper awaits you.

THE CHORUS

Supper, supper, supper awaits us!
No, really, no host
Receives more richly!

(They go out.)

(*Il touche l'épaule d'OLYMPIA.*)

OLYMPIA.

Oui.

SPALANZANI

Vous voyez, jusque là
Voulez vous me faire la grâce
De tenir compagnie à mon OLYMPIA?

HOFFMANN

O bonheur!

SPALANZANI (*à part, riant*).

Nous verrons ce qu'il lui chantera.

NICKLAUSSE (*a SPALANZANI*).

Elle ne soupe pas.

SPALANZANI

Non!

NICKLAUSSE (*à part*).

Ame poetique!

(*SPALANZANI passe derrière OLYMPIA. On entend le bruit d'un ressort.*)

Plaît-il?

SPALANZANI

Rien! la physique! ah monsieur, la physique!

(*Il conduit OLYMPIA à un fauteuil et sort avec les invites.*)

COCHENILLE

Le souper vous attend.

LE CHOEUR (*avec enthousiasm*).

Le souper, le souper, le souper nous attend!
Non, ancun hôte vraiment,
Ne reçoit plus richement!

HOFFMANN

They are at last gone. Ah, I breathe!
Alone, alone, the two of us (*approaching OLYMPIA*);
I have so many things to say,
Oh my Olympia! Let me admire you!
With your charming looks let me intoxicate myself.

(*He touches her shoulder*).

OLYMPIA

Yes.

HOFFMANN

Is it not a dream born of fever?
I thought I heard a sigh escape your lips!

(*He again touches her shoulder*).

OLYMPIA

Yes.

HOFFMANN

Sweet avowal, pledge of our love,
You are mine, our hearts are united forever!
Ah! understand you, tell me, this eternal joy
Of silent hearts.
Living, with but one soul and with same stroke of wing,
Rush up to heaven!
Let, let, my flame
Show you the light of day!
Let your soul open
To the rays of love.

(*He presses OLYMPIA's hand. She rises and walks up and down, then exits.*)

You escape me?... What have I done.
You do not answer?...
Speak! Have I wounded you? Ah!
I'll follow your steps!

(*As HOFFMANN is about to rush out NICKLAUSSE appears.*)

NICKLAUSSE

Here, by Jove, moderate your zeal!
Do you want us to drink without you?...

HOFFMANN

Ils se sont éloignes enfin! Ah je respire!
Seuls, seuls, tous deux!

(*S'approchant d'OLYMPIA.*)

Oue j'ai de choses à te dire,
O mon Olympia! Laisse moi t'admirer!
De ton regard charmant laisse moi m'enivrer.

(*Il touche légèrement l'épaule d'OLYMPIA.*)

OLYMPIA.

Oui.

HOFFMANN

N'est—ce pas un rêve enfanté par la fièvre?
J'ai cru voir un soupir s'échapper de ta lèvre!

(*Il touche de nouveau l'épaule d'OLYMPIA.*)

OLYMPIA.

Oui.

HOFFMANN

Doux aveu, gage de nos amours,
Tu m'appartieus, nos coeurs sont unis pour toujours!
Ah comprends-tu, dis moi, cette joie éternelle
Des coeurs silencieux?
Vivants, n'être qu'une âme, et du même coup d'aile
Nous élancer aux cieux!
Laisse, laissema flamme
Verser en toi le jour!
Laisse éclore ton âme
Aux rayons de l'amour!

(*Il presse la main d'OLYMPIA. Celle ci se léve, parcourt la scène et sort.*)

Tu me fuis? qu'ai je fait? Tu ne me réponds pas.
Parle! t'ai-je irritee? ah je suivrai tes pas!

(*HOFFMANN s'élance, NICKLAUSSE parait.*)

NICKLAUSSE

Eh morbleu, modére ton zèle!
Veux-tu qu'on se grise sans toi?...

Hoffmann's (tenor Gerard Powers) magical glasses trick his mind and heart into falling in love with the automaton Olympia (soprano Georgia Jarman).

Sumi Jo as Olympia in the Los Angeles Opera 2002 production of
Les contes d'Hoffmann

HOFFMANN (*half crazy*)

Nicklausse, I am beloved by her.
Loved! By all the gods.

NICKLAUSSE

By my faith
If you knew what they are saying of your beauty!

HOFFMANN

What can they say? What?

NICKLAUSSE

That she is dead.

HOFFMANN

Great Heavens!

NICKLAUSSE

Or is not of this life.

HOFFMANN (*exalted*)

Nicklausse! I am beloved by her!
Loved! By all the gods.

COPPÉLIUS (*entering, furious*)

Thief! brigand! what a tumble!
Elias is bankrupt!
But I shall find the opportunity
To revenge myself... Robbed!... Me!
I'll kill somebody.

(*Coppelius slips into OLYMPIA's room.*)

(*Everybody enters.*)

SPALANZANI

Here come the waltzers.

COCHENILLE

Here comes the round dance.

HOFFMANN

'Tis the waltz that calls us.

HOFFMANN (*avec ivresse*).

Nicklausse! Je suis aimé d'elle!
Aimié!... Dieu puissant.

NICKLAUSSE

Par ma foi
Si tu savais ce qu'on dit de ta belle!

HOFFMANN

Qu'en peut on dire? Quoi?

NICKLAUSSE

Qu'elle est morte.

HOFFMANN

Juste ciel!

NICKLAUSSE

Ou ne fut pas en vie.

HOFFMANN

Nicklausse! je suis aimé d'elle
Aimé! Dieu puissant.

(*Il sort. NICKLAUSSE le suit.*)

COPPÉLIUS (*entrant, furieaux*).

Voleur! brigand! quelle déroute!
Elias à fait banqueronte!
Va, je saurai trouver le moment opportun
Pour me venger... Volé! moi!... Je tuerai quelqu'un.

(*COPPÉLIUS se glisse dans la chambre d'OLYMPIA.*)

(*Entre tout-le-monde.*)

SPALANZANI

Voici les valseurs.

COCHENILLE

Voici la ritournelle.

HOFFMANN

C'est la valse qui nous appelle.

SPALANZANI (*to OLYMPIA*).

Take the hand of the gentleman, my child.

(*Touching her shoulder.*)

Come.

OLYMPIA

Yes.

(*HOFFMANN takes OLYMPIA and they waltz. They disappear on left.*)

CHORUS

She dances!
In cadence.
'Tis marvelous,
Prodigious,
Room, room,
She passes
Through the air
Like lightning.

THE VOICE OF HOFFMANN (*outside*).

Olympia!

SPALANZANI

Stop them!

THE CHORUS

Who of us will do it?

NICKLAUSSE

She will break his head.

(*HOFFMANN and OLYMPIA re-appear. NICKLAUSSE rushes to stop them.*)

A thousand devils!

(*He is violently struck and falls in an arm chair.*)

THE CHORUS

Patatra!...

SPALANZANI (*à OLYMPIA*).

Prends la main de monsieur, mon enfant.

(*Lui touchant l'épaule.*)

Allons!

OLYMPIA.

Oui.

(*HOFFMANN enlace la taille d'OLYMPIA et ils disparaissent a gauche.*)

LE CHOEUR.

Elle danse!
En cadence!
C'est merveilleux!
Prodigieux!
Place, place!
Elle passe
Elle fend l'air
Comme un éclair.

LA VOIX D'HOFFMANN (*dans la coulisse*).

Olympia!

SPALANZANI

Qu'on les arrête!

LE CHOEUR.

Qui de nous les arrêtera?

NICKLAUSSE

Elle va lui casser la tête!...

(*HOFFMANN et OLYMPIA reparaissent et redescendent.*)

(*NICKLAUSSE s'elance pour les arrétèr.*)

Eh, mille diables!...

(*Il est violemment bausculé et tombe sur un fauteuil.*)

LE CHOEUR.

Patatra!

SPALANZANI (*jumping in*).

Halt!

(*He touches OLYMPIA on the shoulder. She stops suddenly. HOFFMANN, exhausted, falls on a sofa*).

There!

(*To OLYMPIA*) Enough, enough, my child.

OLYMPIA

Yes.

SPALANZANI

No more waltzing.

OLYMPIA

Yes.

SPALANZANI (*to COCHENILLE*).

You, Cochenille,
Take her back.

(*He touches OLYMPIA.*)

COCHENILLE (*pushing OLYMPIA*).

Go on, Go!

OLYMPIA

Yes.

(*Going out, slowly, pushed by COCHENILLE*)

Ha, ha, ha, ha, ha, ha, ha!

THE CHORUS

What can we possibly say?
'Tis an exquisite girl,
She wants in nothing,
She does very well!

NICKLAUSSE (*dolorous voice, pointing to HOFFMANN*).

Is he dead?

SPALANZANI (*examining HOFFMANN*).

No! in fact
His eye glass is broken.
He is reviving.

SPALANZANI (*s'élancant*).

Halte là!

(*Il touche OLYMPIA à l'épaule. Elle s'arrête subitement. HOFFMANN étourdi tombe sur un canapé.*)

SPALANZANI

Voilà!

(*à OLYMPIA.*)

Assez, assez, ma fille.

OLYMPIA.

Oui.

SPALANZANI

Il ne faut plus valser.

OLYMPIA.

Oui.

SPALANZANI (*a COCHENILLE*).

Toi Cochenille,
Reconduis-la.

(*Il touche OLYMPIA.*)

COCHENILLE (*poussant OLYMPIA*).

Va donc. Va!

OLYMPIA.

Oui.

(*En sortant, poussé par COCHENILLE.*)

Ha, ha, ha, ha, ha, ha, ha, ha!

LE CHOEUR.

Que voulez vous qu'on dise?
C'est une fille exquise,
Il ne lui manque rien, Elle est très bien!

NICKLAUSSE (*d'une voix dolente, en montrant HOFFMANN*)

Est-il mort?

SPALANZANI (*examinant HOFFMANN*).

Non, en somme, Son lorgnon seul est en débris
Il reprend ses esprits.

THE CHORUS

Poor young man!

COCHENILLE (*outside*).

Ah!

(*He enters, very agitated.*)

SPALANZANI

What?

COCHENILLE

The man with the glasses... there!

SPALANZANI

Mercy! Olympia!...

HOFFMANN

Olympia!...

(*Sound of breaking springs with much noise*).

SPALANZANI

Ah, heaven and earth, she is broken!

HOFFMANN

Broken!

COPPÉLIUS (*entering*).

Ha, ha, ha, ha, yes. Smashed!

(*HOFFMANN rushes out. SPALANZANI and COPPÉLIUS go at each other, fighting.*)

SPALANZANI

Rascal!

COPPÉLIUS.

Robber!

SPALANZANI

Brigand!

COPPÉLIUS.

Pagan!

SPALANZANI

Bandit!

LE CHŒUR.

Pauvre jeune homme!

COCHENILLE (*dans la coulisse*)

Ah!

(*Il entre, la figure bouleversée.*)

SPALANZANI

Quoi?

COCHENILLE

L'homme aux lunettes ... là.

SPALANZANI

Miséricorde! Olympia!

HOFFMANN

Olympia!

(*On entend un bruit de réssorts qui se brisent avec fracas.*)

SPALANZANI

Ah! terre et cieux! Elle est cassée!

HOFFMANN

Cassée!

Coppelius (*entrant*).

Ha, ha, ha, ha, oui, Fracasseé.

(*HOFFMANN s'élance et disparaît. SPALANZANI et COPPÉLIUS se jettent l'un sur l'autre.*)

SPALANZANI

Gredin!

COPPÉLIUS.

Voleur!

SPALANZANI

Brigand!

COPPÉLIUS.

Païen.

SPALANZANI

Bandit.

COPPÉLIUS.

Pirate!

HOFFMANN (*pale and terror stricken*).

An automaton, an automaton.

(*He falls into an armchair. General laughter.*)

THE CHORUS

Ha, ha, ha, the bomb has burst,
He loved an automaton.

SPALANZANI (*despairingly*).

My automaton.

ALL

An automaton,
Ha, ha, ha, ha!

COPPÉLIUS.

Pirate!

HOFFMANN (*pale et épouvanté*).

Un automate! Un automate!

(*Il tombe sur un fauteuil. Eclat de rire général.*)

LE CHOEUR.

Ha, ha, ha, la bombe éclate
Il aimait un automate!

SPALANZANI (*avec désespoir*).

Mon automate!

TOUS

Un automate!
Ha, ha ha, ha!

Jacques Offenbach (1819–1880)

BARCAROLLE - INTERMEZZO

From "The Tales of Hoffmann," by JACQUES OFFENBACH.

Printed in Great Britain
by Amazon.co.uk, Ltd.,
Marston Gate.